"LOOK OUT! OUTRIDER!"

Julie never noticed the big, black, two-year-old colt when he bolted. She didn't even hear the warning cries. Too late, she saw the impending collision and tried desperately to rein Moriarity out of the path of the fear-crazed colt. She was not fast enough. The full force of a twelve-hundred-pound thoroughbred traveling at forty miles an hour smashed headlong into Julie and her pony. They all crumped to the ground together in a horrible chaos of tangled legs, leather, bodies.

There was no way of escape for Julie. She could only lie there as the beasts scrambled and thrashed. She couldn't possibly avoid the great black hoof that smashed heavily down on her back, driving her deep into darkness. . . .

BARBARA VAN TUYL has raised, bred, ridden, and shown horses most of her life. In addition to the popular "Bonnie" Series, she has written several other non-fiction books about horses. She now lives on a farm in Maryland.

SIGNET Young Adult Books You'll
Enjoy Reading

The Betrayal
of Bonnie

by Barbara Van Tuyl

A SIGNET BOOK
NEW AMERICAN LIBRARY
TIMES MIRROR

SIGNET, SIGNET CLASSICS, MENTOR, PLUME AND MERIDIAN BOOKS
are published by The New American Library, Inc.,
1301 Avenue of the Americas, New York, New York 10019

FIRST PRINTING, MAY, 1975

4 5 6 7 8 9

PRINTED IN THE UNITED STATES OF AMERICA

For my sister, Gail Appel—a really special person—and for her pinto, Will-E-Do, a special, spotted horse.

Chapter *ONE*

The slim blond girl perched lightly in the irons, her graceful body moving in perfect harmony with the pulsing cadence of the galloping horse beneath her. She rode as a part of that flying, surging motion: at one with the thrusting power, she seemed as necessary as the flashing hoofs that skimmed the track and devoured distance with incredible ease. The wind tore at the black mane, whipping its strands against her cheeks; rushing in her ears, it drowned all other noise save the rhythmic drum-drum-drum of those pounding feet.

To the east, the sky was only beginning to turn in its bed of shadow, casting off the blue-gray coverlet of night to expose the rose-tinted sheets of dawn. In minutes now the gentle creeping light would glow, then spark, then catch fire as the horizon burst forth with the glory of sunrise.

Monty Everett leaned on the outside rail, studying the pair intently through high-powered binoculars. The last of the night mist hung in great smoky patches, or rolled like cotton-candy tumbleweeds along the earth. As the girl and the horse rounded the turn, they were trans-

formed for an instant to an inky silhouette printed stark
against the deepening pink of the sky. They were a striking spectacle indeed, suspended there above the ground
as though by the swirling haze. Then, gradually, they
took on dimension and color as they lost the angle of
light from behind.

The great wash of dawn light, the perfection of motion before it, would have tempted any artist to reach
for his brushes, but the young man had no eye for the
beauty of the morning's colors. He was watching the
horse. Deliberately, diligently, to the exclusion of all
else, he had absorbed himself in the flowing stride of the
magnificent bay mare. Critical of every move, he
searched for flaws and found none. So intent was this
scrutiny of his that he never heard the approaching foot-
steps, and was taken unawares by the voice at his elbow.

"Mornin', boss." The voice was cheerful. "They do
look pretty out there."

Monty jumped, lowered his glasses. "Morning,
Scorchy. Taking a horseman's holiday? I thought this
was your day off."

"I am and it is," said the smaller man. "But it isn't
too often I get to see the big mare work. Always seem to
be someplace else when she's goin' out. Peaches asked
me to bring up her cooler, too. I hung it on the fence at
the gap." He gestured at the walkway that led off the
training track, where a folded woolen cover was draped
over the rail.

"Thanks. It's cool yet, and I wouldn't want Bonnie to
catch a cold *now*." Monty shivered slightly, at the
thought or at the morning chill, and hunched further
into his turtleneck sweater.

"Sure would like to see her run," muttered Scorchy
half to himself. "D'you think she's gonna make it, boss?
I mean—all the way? I'm the only one here at Deepwater that's never seen her in action. I was still in Cali-

fornia when she was tearin' up the tracks and hangin' up all them funny fractions for t'others to shoot at."

"Even so, you seem to be a paid-up member of the Sunbonnet fan club. It doesn't take long around here," Monty grinned, "with the president and founder in residence."

"Why, I'd be president myself if 'tweren't for all those others ahead of me! If I never get to see her run for real, even, I'm proud just to know her. Can't imagine where else I'd be able to meet a four-hundred-thousand-dollar yearling that got horsenapped, played for a ringer, rescued, then went on to win more'n half a million and be voted a filly of the year, all in one package. In fact——"

"Whoa, Scorchy! I'm part of the club too, remember. A charter member at that; nobody thinks more of that big girl than I do, except Julie herself." He raised the glasses, picking up the horse and rider just short of the mile marker. As they passed the blue-and-white pole, the girl stood up, allowing the mare to gallop steadily for another eighth of a mile before easing her back; at the three-quarter pole she pulled up completely, turned and jogged back toward the gap.

"She's looking better every day. I think you may get your wish. But Scorchy," he added seriously, "don't repeat that to Julie. I don't want her setting her heart on Bonnie running again, only to find out she can't make it."

The two men turned and walked down the track to meet the bay who had made such a mark on racing history and the young lady who was wholly responsible for her fabulous career. "Boss, it's like a storybook to me. I mean, me, Scorchy L. Grayson, walkin' out to meet Sunbonnet *and* Julie Jefferson, just like they weren't famous or anything."

"They're the fugitives from a gothic novel, not you,

Scorch. You couldn't dream up the things that have happened to them if you were a smart little old woman with a quill pen. . . . I only hope that there's a happy ending planned."

Monty picked up the cooler and shook out its folds as he waited for the horse to cover the last hundred feet. Julie, he saw, was positively glowing as she pulled up.

"How'd she look, Monty? She felt super! Hi, Scorchy, what are you doing here today? Honestly, she's feeling so good that I was afraid she'd break off and breeze a half before I could pull her up, and she never quit playing till we'd gone a mile, but I kidded her out of it on the second time round—when can I turn her loose and let her run? Just a little way, I mean? She's only humoring me now, you know." Julie dropped lightly to earth, in fact if not in conversation, and reached for the cooler to cover the mare. "See, she hasn't even turned a hair, and she isn't breathing hard enough to blow out a match!" Julie patted the sleek neck as she lifted the reins over Bonnie's ears and slipped them into the crook of her arm.

"I'll take her back if you want," Scorchy said. "There's coffee and doughnuts in the tack room, still warm from the bakery."

"Oh thanks, Scorchy, that sounds lovely. I'll be out to walk her myself in a sec. Now, Monty, tell me what you really think. Be accurate and truthful. Is Bonnie going to race again?" she demanded, linking her arm in his. "Talk!"

"Edgewise?"

"I'll keep shut."

"Well, remembering that it's the first I've seen of her since you brought her over from Fieldstone, I'll say she looks better than I've ever seen her, and it doesn't seem —the ankle, that is—to be troubling her. I can't say anything for certain till——"

"You can't say anything for certain, ever, without hedging it in with *ifs* and *buts* and *in cases!*"

"Till we've let her work a couple of times and X-ray the fracture site again," said Monty firmly. "If she works back to her old form, and Dr. Haffner says she's okay, then I don't see anything to stop her." He was encouraging her, exactly as he'd asked Scorchy not to do, but a genuine enthusiasm brought on by watching the great mare was not to be held back, however protective he wanted to be with this girl. "Why don't you plan to work a quarter next Sunday? Think you can keep her under wraps till then?"

"Sure I can," said Julie, with the confidence born of that total understanding she shared with her horse, an understanding that had never been misplaced. "Bonnie may not like it much, but she won't run off with me, and I'll explain to her——"

"Julie!"

"I will! You *know* she understands me!"

"Yes, I guess she does, in a way," Monty said, giving in.

"I will explain to her that another week of galloping is doctor's orders. In fact, we'll discuss it right now, while we're walking on the ring." She automatically began searching her pockets for gumdrops, Bonnie's special treat. "You could bring me some coffee and a doughnut if you had the energy," she said, and hurried off.

Monty went into the tack room and collected their breakfast, sighing a little. He had long since accepted the fact that Bonnie came first, but he still wished that occasionally he, Monty, devoted, faithful Monty, might claim her undivided attention. It wasn't impossible, it surely couldn't be impossible? But to accomplish it, he needed words to tell her what was on his mind, in his heart . . . and on that subject Montgomery Everett, who had never been in love with anyone in his entire life but Julie Jefferson, was as hopelessly tongue-tied as a bashful lad out of the summer of 1875.

Only when the big mare had been completely cooled out at the walking ring, watered off, and brushed until her dark bay hide returned the morning sunlight, did Julie feel that she was free to leave. If the young trainer often thought that she was being overly concerned about the horse, that in fact she had built the larger part of her own life around Bonnie, he had only to remember the last few years in order to feel thoroughly ashamed of his jealousy: to recall how she'd found the starving, sick creature, brought her home, discovered that she was no ordinary horse; then proved Bonnie's real identity and fought through a web of lies and miles of red tape so she could race, finally exposing the complex criminal scheme that had stolen the highest-priced yearling ever sold from her multimillionaire owner, Rollin Tokov.

And the troubles and, well, "adventures" was the only word, hadn't stopped there. The girl and her gallant mare had been through tragedy and triumph, in a brilliant racing career punctuated by a series of unique events that often made Monty believe that the Fates were playing entirely too fast and loose with them. Just when everything was at last going smoothly for them, said Fates reached out and flicked their dirty old fingernails at the wonder horse in mid-stride, with a fractured bone in her ankle. That had been late in her four-year-old season. Now, with two years of rest behind her (during which she'd been bred and produced a set of twins), they were trying again. Trying to bring her back once more to the racing that was the beat of her heart. Trying carefully, one day at a time, so as not to hurt her. Trying with their fingers crossed. . . . And when he thought of all this, all they had been through together, Monty knew he couldn't begrudge these two their time together, nor be jealous of the special bond they shared. He could only be glad and grateful that he was a part of their world.

Julie ran the rub rag over Bonnie's gleaming coat one last time, took off her halter, and offered her a solitary gumdrop.

"That's today's last, but I'll have a new supply by tomorrow." The mare accepted the candy and the information with her usual dignity, and gave Julie a playful nudge out of the stall door.

"Sometimes I believe she *does* know what you tell her."

"She does. It's just that she had a little trouble making words—our kind of words—but if only I wasn't so untutored in her language, I could understand what she's saying. . . ."

"I know just how you feel," said Monty, with a look that went right over Julie's bright blond head. "How about the Pancake Shack for a real Sunday lunch? I'm starving."

"We'll have to stop by my quarters and pick up Pushy," she said.

"I invited you, not that tricolored bear! St. Bernards can't sit in chairs, anyway. Not comfortably."

"I won't bring him *in,* I'll only take him along in the car. It's his favorite treat and we haven't been off the farm all week."

"What about the one-dog demolition unit, code name Nana, standard disguise a beagle-suit? How can you leave her without risking a chewed-up chair?"

"She isn't here. She's——"

"Off on another giant rabbit hunt?"

"At Fieldstone with Leon. My marvelous beagle with the very exceptional nose, to which we owe Bonnie's safety as you will recollect if you think about it for a minute, Mr. Witty, strained her back out hunting, and

Leon thought Doc Haffner should keep her under surveillance. He called yesterday to say she's doing fine,
and Doc thinks I can pick her up Friday. So she'll be
here when you arrive on Saturday."

"As long as it isn't her nose that's damaged. Ever
think of insuring it?" asked Monty.

"Forget it! There's not enough money available to
safeguard that priceless proboscis!" Julie was always
vehement on the subject of her "poor misunderstood
Nana"—whom Monty understood quite well—and, in
fact, on the subject of all animals.

"Only kidding," said Monty mildly. "Pushy and pan-
cakes, then."

They stopped by Julie's apartment; this was a couple
of rooms above the carriage house, one of the original
buildings of Deepwater Farm. She dashed up the stairs,
slipped into a clean pair of slacks and a sweater, and
collected the St. Bernard. Pushy was so overcome with
glee at the prospect of riding in the car that he cavorted
all around it before climbing in; and a cavorting Saint is
an awesome thing to see. "Like a gamboling hippo,"
said Monty, very much under his breath, as he drove
out, the huge dog breathing happily down his nape.

By the time they'd eaten, a light rain had begun, and
the morning sun was invisible behind a layer of blacken-
ing clouds. "We'll just miss the worst of it if we hurry,"
Monty said, rolling up the windows. "From the way
those clouds are moving, it won't really pour for another
twenty minutes."

"Have to pick up some gumdrops for Bonnie, but I'll
be quick."

He stopped at the drugstore; Julie hurried in, made
her vital purchase and ran back to the car, while pon-
derous raindrops splattered the pavement and struck
with dull little thumps on the windshield. The breeze
was rapidly gaining strength, and within minutes was a

strong wind driving the water relentlessly at them in a solid, colorless curtain. Monty slowed to a creep and pulled on his lights in an effort to see and be seen. He could not see much.

"Think of it as violets," said Julie when he'd growled for the third time.

"Ho, ho, ho," said Monty heavily, straining to follow the road through a perfect river of rain. Somehow he got them almost home; then, abruptly, a flash of silver-white light burst jaggedly before them, there was an explosion of sound, and the electrical display began. Through skillful driving, a good knowledge of the road, and some fair guesswork, Monty skidded along at seven or eight miles an hour, his eyes tensely on the route before him. Just before the Deepwater turnoff, all his senses concentrating on their safety and progress, he missed the slight movement off the right sand shoulder, but Julie did not.

"Monty! Stop! There's something alive there!" With the girl, to think it was to do it, and before a startled Monty could pump the brakes or ask what it was, she had pulled the door handle, leaped out of the crawling car, and was running back along the edge of the road. Monty brought the car to a halt as quickly as he could, slewing sideways a little, the open door flapping in the rain. He slid over and got out, pushed the excited St. Bernard back, tried to close the door, pushed Pushy again, fell to his knees in the muck, scrambled up and shoved Pushy violently into the back seat one final time, slammed the door. Praying that no automobiles were close behind, and that he was far enough off to the side to be safe from any possible traffic, he followed Julie.

She was kneeling in the drainage ditch, soaked through, trying fiercely to lift something from the ground—something alive.

"Oh, Monty, he's hurt, and he's just a puppy but he's too big for me!" There were tears mixing with the rain on her upturned face. "He's cold, too. Can you pick him up?"

"Did we hit him?" asked Monty, horrified, kneeling beside her.

"No, no! I saw him by a lightning flash. He was right here."

"Wait with him, I'll back the car up, we'll put him on the big mat and slide him in over the tailgate." He sprinted, slipping and flailing his arms to keep upright, to the car. He fought Pushy, who still wanted to come out and see; backed up and got out. "Can't tell how he's hurt, so the less we move him, the better." Together they eased the stricken dog into the cargo space, Pushy going wild but staying back at Julie's sharp command. Julie appropriated Monty's emergency blanket from the second seat and wrapped it gently around the animal, which was shuddering violently.

Without hesitation or discussion, Monty swung the car around and headed for town and the closest veterinarian's office. A phone call brought the doctor to his clinic on the double, despite the abominable weather and the Sunday day off. After what seemed an age to Julie, the dog was resting, tranquilized, with one hind leg in a cast and both forepaws shaved, treated, and bandaged.

"Hit by a car or a motorcycle," the vet had told them. "A few hours ago, too. Lucky for this pup that you spotted him out there, or he'd have died from shock and exposure. Still in poor shape. I'll want to keep him a week or ten days, see how he does. I can probably leave the front legs open by then. Cast'll have to stay on for six weeks at least, but we'll fret over that when the time comes. Why don't you call in the morning to see how he's making out?"

Their damp clothes got soaking wet again as they ran out and piled into the car, where Pushy had gone to sleep. "A few hours, he said!" shrilled Julie, indignant, and woke the St. Bernard with a start. "Monty, did you hear him? That puppy was struck before it even began to rain. And they *left* him there! How can people do such things? How could they drive on and not *care?* And what will we do with him when he's better?"

"Whatever you think is right, honey. Put an ad in the Found column of the local papers, see if his owners turn up. I'm no expert on dogs, but I think he's an expensive breed—Irish wolfhound or Scottish deerhound, and pure-bred too, I'll bet."

"If nobody claims him, I'll keep him myself. Did you ever see such a dear face, except for Pushy's and Nana's, naturally?"

"And dozens of others you could name. Julie, do you have any conception of how big that dog will be within a year?"

"Twice the size of Push! I don't know. I don't care. I can't send him on his lonesome way, can I? And you don't seem to want him—"

"I'd like to have him," said Monty, "but you can't coop a big dog in an apartment all day, and they don't allow any dogs on the track grounds, so what would he do? Get a job? Of course *you* could keep him, and he'd probably be eternally grateful that he'd been an accident victim, but you can't adopt every stray animal that wanders into your life. At the rate you're going lately, girl, you'll soon qualify as an animal shelter."

She turned a face toward him whose radiance was not quite lost in the gray dimness of the leaden, rainy day. "Oh, Monty, what a splendid idea!"

"What idea?"

She had seized a thought and was laying plans for its completion, in her customary agile fashion. "Being an animal shelter. What an inspiration! I could be, I mean I could run, a sort of halfway house for strays, and injured animals, and ones that needed homes. An animal placement bureau. What a perfect career! Naturally I'll keep this *one* dog with me, but I could place all the others."

" 'Could' is the operative word. 'Wouldn't' is more accurate," said Monty. "You'd keep this one, then the next one, and every one until you couldn't find room for one more; then you'd move to larger quarters—brother! You might christen it 'Dogs and Cats Keep.' "

"Like the stronghold in medieval castles where all the valuables were kept?"

"No. As in 'Dogs and Cats Keep Pouring In.' Don't I know you, Miss J!"

"That's not fair, really. I found homes for all eight of Marguerite's kittens last time, and that beautiful black dog that wandered in at Fieldstone, and Miko's dachshund when they discovered her brother was allergic to him, and the gray fluffy cat that kept misplacing her kittens, and plenty of others. Wait and see! This is the best idea you've had yet." She leaned toward him. "You'll help, won't you, Monty? That is, whenever you're home, and not busy?"

"I'll be delighted." Monty knew when he was outnumbered. And Julie, after all, could have talked him into an ostrich-farming project if she'd really tried. Whatever she wanted was fine with him, however he kidded her; and with or without his encouragement, she'd go ahead with this latest in her series of animal-oriented schemes.

"You're a dear," said Julie, settling back as comfortably as soppy clothes and dripping hair would allow. Pushy leaned forward and put his immense chin and all-enveloping dewlaps on her shoulder. "And Mr. T is a dear, too," she added dreamily.

"Why Mr. T?" This was Rollin Tolkov, owner of Deepwater and Fieldstone, and their employer.

"For allowing me to use part of his land for my animal shelter."

"He's going to do that? I thought you just had the idea *now*."

"I did. No, you did, don't you remember? But he will."

"Will what?" asked Monty, slightly at sea.

"Donate a good site. Or loan it to me, anyway. It's the sort of thing he would do, isn't it? Bless him," said Julie, and stared out at the rain, being thankful that she was surrounded by such good, kind people.

Monty drove on, a little in awe, as usual, of this girl's unbounded faith in her friends. . . .

Chapter TWO

Next Friday morning, Julie drove to Fieldstone Farm to pick up her mended beagle. Over a sandwich-and-milk lunch, she brought her old gang of cronies up to date on Deepwater doings, particularly Bonnie's progress. Pop's inquiry about Pushy launched the girl into an account of the Sunday rainstorm and her discovery of the big injured puppy.

"But some good's going to come of it, and it's all Monty's idea!" At this both Leon and Stash sat up and exchanged *uh-oh!* stares across the table; an announcement by Julie delivered with that kind of enthusiasm and attributed to Monty was almost certain to be a Julie Project reluctantly okayed by the young trainer—positively so if it had to do with animals.

"What did inventive ol' Monty originate that's worked you up that way?" asked Stash innocently.

"He thought I might become an animal shelter."

"Why not an elm tree?" said Pop in his machine-gun style. "Why not a good trout stream? Why an animal shelter?"

"Why not a bride?" Leon murmured.

"Oh, you know what I mean. He gave me the idea for starting one, and I spoke to Mr. T about it and he said I could have two acres off the far side of the yearling pasture (your yearling pasture, Stash, but you don't honestly need that part, do you?). Then he said I could no way touch any of the money that Bonnie's already won, because it's all invested for me for later; but that anything she wins now can go toward building the shelter, and he'd fix it so there'd be a small, steady income for expenses and upkeep and I can even advertise a little. People will bring me the animals they find, or don't want, and I'll place them in new homes that truly *care* for them, and won't it be great?"

Everyone agreed that the concept was wonderful, while privately wondering how Julie Jefferson could find that many extra hours in the days that had always been so full for her.

"But if Bonnie doesn't make it all the way?" asked Leon gently, peering over his glasses at her. "What if she doesn't run again? You given thought to ways of raising all the money you'd need if that occurred?"

In the abrupt silence, Julie frowned, bit her lip, then gave a quick shrug of dismissal. "No, I haven't. But any other way of raising funds would take too long. There's a real need around here for a center like this. Bonnie will run, Leon; I know she will. She tells me every morning with each step she takes. She's better now—I know it's a miracle, but it's true—better than she ever was! When she runs, she'll win."

Lunch ended on this positive note. Julie collected Nana, then paid a long visit to Tam and Deerstalker, Bonnie's twins; collected a few clothes and sundries, loaded her little station wagon and drove back to Deepwater and Bonnie.

The following evening Monty arrived and heard all about the desperate need for a good animal shelter. Julie had discovered that the small local humane society was closed, and unavailable for even emergency phone calls, from Saturday noons till Monday mornings. "That's one thing that'll never be said of *our* establishment!" said the girl, her big blue eyes snapping angrily. "Twenty-four-hour phone service, if I have to sit there myself right beside it!" She went on to elaborate on Mr. T's cooperation, and tell Monty of the restrictions placed on her sources of funds.

As it had been with Leon, the first thought that went through Monty's mind was of what would happen to her newest dream if the big mare didn't make a successful comeback. That would mean that what seemed to be Julie's two paramount hopes—to see Bonnie run again, win again, and to establish a good animal shelter— would both be blasted. He said nothing, however. No use predicting that unlaid eggs would be rotten. Tomorrow he'd have a better idea of how things stood, when he'd watched Bonnie work. It would only be a quarter mile, not much of a distance, but he'd learn as much as possible until he saw Doc Haffner's radiographs. Then he'd know for certain.

They waited until the sky was light, even bright, before walking the powerful mare onto the track. She seemed well aware of something unusual in the offing; she jigged and danced in small circles, while Monty somewhat nervously rattled off his instructions one final time.

"Back her up to the quarter pole, let her gallop an easy mile and breeze the final quarter to the wire. Try not to let her get away from you, and ease her up as soon as you can. Okay?"

"Right!" Julie steadied the excited beast with a calming hand on the silken neck. As always, she was nerved up herself at the prospect of riding one of the fleetest Thoroughbreds, *her* Thoroughbred, after all!—one of the fleetest in racing history; and did her best not to communicate too much of her own tension to her mount.

She turned the mare to the left, heading up the race-track in the wrong direction, and jogged slowly toward the quarter pole. There she turned and broke off, set-tling easily into a steady gallop. The horse was leaning into the bit, waiting for the signal that would mean she was free to stretch out and run, hoofs barely touching the dirt, fantastic stride eating distance.

As they reached the halfway marker, Julie felt an electric tingle run up her spine. In less than a quarter of a mile—two furlongs—she would begin to let the horse move up, increase her already lengthening stride, and in that moment the mare would know that it was time. Two or three jumps from the all-important quarter marker the girl would turn loose a thousand pounds of pent-up equine energy, and they would pass that pole running. Julie knew there'd be no chance to restrain Bonnie once she understood what was being asked of her. She was not very confident that she'd be able to pull her up after only a quarter of a mile.

The pole seemed to close in on them; the girl felt the mare tensed beneath her, every atom of that great fluid body poised for the approaching flight. Ten strides, five strides, she crouched a little nearer to the straining mus-cles of the satin neck. Three strides, she folded up com-pletely, changing the feel of her hands on the reins from that of active resistance to one of total participation. In a single heartbeat the horse became a blur of flying rich-red-brown speed incarnate, half a ton of deter-mined hurricane roaring toward the finish line.

In seconds it was over, and a stride past the wire Julie stood up in her irons and began talking to the horse. Bonnie heard, reluctantly checked the flaming pace that she'd set for herself. Despite her devotion for Julie, her genuine desire to comply with the girl's every request, more than half another mile flew by before she brought herself to a halt and allowed Julie to turn her back toward the gap. As they approached the three men waiting there, Julie tried to read an answer on their faces, but the eyes that held on the sweat-darkened beast were unreadable.

Monty Everett at last hauled his gaze from the returning horse, to stare once again, disbelieving, at the stopwatch in his damp hand.

"It isn't true," he said blankly. "I had hopes, but this can't be right. Twenty and two-fifths seconds." He turned to Scorchy and Peaches. "Bonnie just *worked* a quarter faster than most horses *run!*" he said in the jargon of the track: "run" being used to mean "race" and "worked" meaning "trained." He saw from their expressions that there was nothing wrong with his watch.

Scorchy said, awed, "We got twenty and change, same as you. Man!" he burst out, grinning, "isn't she some kinda horse? I never seen a horse hang up a fraction like this at the track, much less on the farm! I never have to watch her in a race, boss; I seen it all this morning."

Julie hopped down, while eager hands reached to loosen the girth and cover the steaming animal with a cooler. "She was good, wasn't she?"

"Better than good. Better than best. Twenty and two-fifths on a training track with nothing to run against. She wasn't running out there, Julie, she was flying, she had wings. Good land and panther tracks," Monty exclaimed, reverting to the ancient oaths of his boyhood, "if I'd ever had the least notion she'd lay down a work like that, I'd have told you to rate her a bit. It was really too fast for a work."

"I couldn't hold her, Monty! She only waited as long as that out of courtesy to me. She *wants* to run again.

She wanted to go farther today. You saw how long it took her to decide to pull up? Well, then, can she make it all the way, or can't she?"

Monty pulled himself together, wondering briefly whether he was actually shaking all over or only felt like it. "Doc Haffner will take the X-rays tomorrow. If everything looks all right, and she stays as sound as she seems now, I say she can make it. It's almost as if she'd been improved by the long rest. I don't understand it, heaven knows, but she always was something special. She's gotten stronger instead of deteriorating. She's getting better with age. She makes track-record moves look easy."

"She is some kinda horse!" said Scorchy.

The mare was carefully cooled out and put away with her legs done up in a mild liniment and standing bandages. And this was the beginning of the tense, hopeful, worrisome, good time.

For four consecutive weeks Monty Everett made the long Saturday drive down from Roxbury Race Course to Deepwater Farm to watch the bay mare work on Sunday. Three-eighths of a mile, then twice at a half; and she made it look like colt's play. Each time she was as good as the time before—no, better, for the distances increased and she grew fitter by the day. Each time she jogged back sound, tossing her head, starched with the pride of her accomplishment, striking the ground full and square with four hoofs that showed no trace of lameness. Each time the Deepwater crew waited with held breath while Doctor Haffner took radiographs of the old fracture site, then let out audible sighs of respite when he read them dry and declared them clean.

The fourth weekend brought the beginning of April and the close of the meeting at Roxbury. On Monday, the Tolkov racing stable would send horses, men, and tack to the familiar stalls of Barn 7 at Kandahar Park, less than thirty miles from their home farm. Roxbury was nice enough, Monty said to himself, but Kandahar was home, and near enough to Deepwater to allow him to commute if he wished. Closer to Deepwater was closer to Julie too.

To keep Julie, insofar as he could, from pinning all her world on hopes that might not prove sound, Monty had carefully maintained a wait-and-see attitude after each of Bonnie's works, and refused to speculate on the mare's racing comeback. However, his professional opinion was optimistic, and long before he left the track on that first April Saturday he had decided that barring unforeseen setbacks, this would be Bonnie's last week at the farm.

As on the three previous Sundays, Monty was not to be disappointed. The fact that he'd stretched the distance out another furlong—five-eighths of a mile—did nothing to alter the animal's performance. In fact, it seemed to him that the farther she went, the better she ran; and when he finally pushed in the stopper of his watch to register the last sizzling fraction, he could only shake his head and wonder what made one particular horse so different from all the others. What secret of mechanical construction lay beneath those rippling muscles, what driving obsession in her brain, that time and again set her apart from her whole breed? All he could answer to that was the horseman's traditional, intangible accolade for a beast of outstanding ability: *class.* And no horse had ever deserved the term more than Bonnie!

From the beginning of her whole saga, Monty had known that she was the answer to every trainer's dream, and was continually grateful that chance had placed such a giant of the turf in his young but capable hands. If she never set hoof on a track again, he'd still had the privilege of training her and watching her win a fortune in purses, forge a record for future fillies to strive toward. . . .

Even now, as she turned and jogged back toward him, he gave a sudden shiver of excitement. He'd watched critically, intently, for any break in the relentless rhythm of her stride, but she would not falter. And in a flash of foresight, in defiance of all the cautious superstitions tied to racing, he knew without doubt that she would race again.

Before Julie's feet hit the ground, Monty was spreading the cooler over Bonnie's neck. In minutes she had been bathed, scraped, covered, and was cooling out on the walking ring.

"Well, then," said Monty, as he walked along beside the girl and the mare, "we'll ship to Kandahar tomorrow morning and take the rest of the day to get set up. Then Dan will go down Tuesday afternoon with the van, to leave Passing Fancy at Fieldstone and Catspaw and Early Mist here for a couple of weeks of rest. You can plan to ship Bonnie back with him on Wednesday morning."

Julie nodded swift assent. "You really think she's ready, don't you? I mean you're pretty sure she'll be okay to run?"

Monty said evenly, "They're running the Marquesa Stakes on May third at Kandahar. For mares, four-year-olds and up, going a mile and a quarter. Nominations closed six weeks ago, and in order to miss a supplemental nomination fee, I entered her—just in case. It doesn't mean that we have to run her; we can always scratch if she isn't in top shape. But I think she will be, and we have thirty-one days to find out."

Julie stared at him, wide-eyed, as the full import of his words registered. Then she hugged him tightly and, whirling, kissed her surprised mare on the nose. "Hear that, Bonnie? We're going to the races! *You're* going, anyway, and I'm helping. Scorchy! Peaches! Did you hear the news! *Bonnie's going back to the races!*"

Chapter THREE

On Wednesday morning, a dawning full of sun and promise, Julie appeared at Bonnie's door as usual, but instead of carrying her exercise saddle and bridle, she brought with her a set of four cottons and four gray flannel bandages. These she stacked neatly in one corner of the stall, while she went about the rituals of grooming the big mare. She curried and brushed the already-gleaming hide until satisfied that it could shine no brighter; then she began wrapping the muscular limbs in cotton and flannel, to guard against injury while Bonnie would be riding in the van.

Begin with the left fore, unwind the neatly rolled cotton so that it lies smoothly on the leg. Good thick bandages—at least five sheets of cotton in each—save a horse from cuts and bruises if he should step on himself with metal shoes, in case the van stops suddenly or the road turns rough. Now the tightly rolled flannel is wrapped snugly over the cotton to hold it in place. No wrinkles to crease or bunch the cotton into lumps against the delicate tendons. Secure with two shiny pins and on to the next leg. Four legs . . . all set.

29

Bonnie watched Julie's activities with mild interest. Bandages were nothing new to her, and if the girl wanted to dress her in them this morning, that was acceptable. It had been long since she'd worn leg wraps, but she remembered them. There was no reason to neglect her taste buds. She wiggled her lips in Julie's hair and gave her a gentle nudge in the pocket.

"Sorry, I wasn't thinking." The girl fished out half a dozen gumdrops and spread them on her palm. "But it's an exciting day, old Bonnet! I thought it might never come, but here it is. Wait till you see where you're going!"

Less than an hour later, the Deepwater van stopped at the stable gate of Kandahar Park. A security guard stepped from the gatehouse. "Morning, Dan. Who've you got aboard this time?"

"Just one. Sunbonnet." Dan Gibson smiled. It certainly would be grand having Bonnie under the shed again.

The guard made a note, waved him through. The van moved slowly into Kandahar.

Julie snapped a lead shank on Bonnie's halter and led her out of the van into the bustle of the backstretch. The big mare stood stock-still for a long moment, letting the familiar sounds and smells wash over her. The hum of a whirlpool tub, the squeak of a hot-walking machine, the pungent whiff of liniments and tonics, medications and sweat; the constant mingling streams of grooms, trainers, exercise boys, hot-walkers, maintenance men, an occasional owner—*racetrack!*

Bonnie flung up her lovely head, let out a clear call, and pranced to the end of the shank. Julie, quite unprepared for this maneuver, had all she could do to restrain the high-stepping, capering horse and pilot her toward her stall.

She barely avoided a mishap outside the number five

barn when a two-year-old pulled back on the hot-walking machine, broke his halter and bolted for his stall, narrowly missing Bonnie. The mare's reaction was instantaneous and in the opposite direction, which nearly ripped the shank out of Julie's hand and did jerk her to her knees. Recovering, she scrambled up, thankful that only Barn 6 stood between them and their destination.

By the time they stepped under the shed in barn seven, Bonnie's glossy coat was black with the sweat of excitement, and Julie could barely keep the dancing horse in hand. She grinned at Beau's hearty greeting and thankfully accepted his offer to give Bonnie a few turns round the shed.

"Whew! You'd think she'd never seen a racetrack before," the girl exclaimed. "Acting like a baby that's green-broke and's never been off the farm. It's going to take ages to get her cooled out. Take a slow turn while I get some water. Pull out next time around and I'll sponge her off."

Beau embraced Bonnie's neck, smearing himself with the sweat. "She's just excited, glad to be back where the action is! Bless her old heart. Come on, you Bonnie-girl, take a walk with Uncle Beau Watkins and tell me what you've been up to, all this long time. We got a stack o' news to catch up with!"

Julie began to fill a bucket. A dark face peered out from beneath the web stall guard across from the water spigots. "Morning, Miss Julie! Just get here? Where's the big horse?"

"Morning, Drop Cord—we just got here this minute and Bonnie's jumping like a hoptoad and lathering herself with the fun of being back. She's wringing wet. Beau's got her and I'm going to give her a quick bath."

"I'll be out to help you in a sec'. Soon's I do this horse up in mud." He went into the stall again to finish applying the wet, poultice-like clay to a horse's shins and ankles.

Two baths and a number of trips around the shed were necessary before Bonnie had settled down enough to be put in her stall. Even then she would grab a mouthful of hay from the back of her stall and prance to the door while she ate, plainly afraid of missing some important occurrence. She was home!

"I hope she calms down by tomorrow," Julie said fervently to the young jockey, Beau. "If she keeps on like this, I'll *never* stay in the middle of her."

Now Monty joined them. All business, he stared at Bonnie a moment, then said, "Julie, you can gallop her for the rest of the week, give her an easy work on Monday, then hand over the reins to Beau for the three weeks before the Marquesa. Beau can take Moriarty along with you, and then you can ride him out with Beau when you switch. After all, he was originally Bonnie's pony and I wouldn't want to disappoint her."

"Hey, where is Moriarty anyway?" Julie's face lit with an inspiration. "I haven't seen him yet, and I bet he could quiet her."

"Marsh has him over to the blacksmith shop," volunteered Drop Cord. "Ought to be comin' back any minute."

On cue precisely, the good-tempered racetrack pony appeared under the shed in company with Marshall Droll, another Deepwater exercise boy. It took Bonnie only a minute to recognize his distinctive brown-and-white coat, and with a loud whinny of welcome, she thrust her head over her door and extended her neck to its limit. The two old friends touched noses and exchanged playful nips; then Bonnie, satisfied at last that all was as it should be, returned to the corner of her stall and settled down to serious eating.

"Cast your eye on that, will you!" said Drop Cord.

"One word with old Mori and she's happy as a clam at high tide. Couldn't be contented till everybody was accounted for." He ambled off toward the tack room, to return shortly with a small bottle which he set down outside the stall. "I'll give her another ten minutes and then rub her down with this," he said to Monty. "It'll keep her muscles from getting stiff or tying up after that spell of excitement she had."

"What is it, Drop Cord?" asked Julie, eyeing the bottle with a suggestion of doubt.

"One of my special remedies. I mix it myself. Doctor Lejeune, he taught me how to make most of my remedies, but they all had funny foreign names on 'em that I couldn't say rightly, so I gave 'em numbers. This is number eleven."

"How many are there altogether?" asked Monty.

"If you count all the variations, thirty-three."

"And you make them all from memory?" The girl was incredulous.

"Oh, it's easy," said the big man, embarrassed by her awe. "I worked for old Doc for more'n fifteen years. Him and me was the only ones ever touched our medicines in all that time. He taught me careful, so I could do 'em blindfolded, and still could."

Monty winked at his head groom and said to Julie, "Don't you worry about Drop Cord. He's the best leg man on the track, bar none, and having him here is like having a resident vet. I keep asking him innocent little questions, trying to pick his brains, hoping that one of these days he'll slip and give away a trade secret or two; but I don't know any more after two years than I did on his first day with us. All I know is that my horses were never as sound and healthy before he come to us."

"Oh, now, I'm nothin' but a simple old country doctor with a satchelful o' herbs and roots," said Drop

Cord, scuffing his toe along the ground. He and Monty looked at each other and chuckled.

Julie was to remember that brief scene, much later, with qualms of anxiety.

Now, reluctantly, she took herself away from the shed's activities and headed, with a little prodding from Monty, toward the track kitchen and a late breakfast. Outside the doors, a small and nondescript puppy sat hungrily sniffing the delicious odors that drifted from within, his upturned face silently begging for recognition, a stump of a tail thudding on the packed ground.

"Oh, Monty, isn't he adorable?" Julie was on her knees, a twelve-year-old again at once, petting the wriggling furball that was instantly responsive to her gentle touch. "Who's he belong to? Do you suppose he's lost?"

"No I do *not*," said Monty quickly, seeing the warning signs of still another dog in Julie's small apartment. "You know they don't allow dogs in the kitchen—his owner's having breakfast, the lucky man."

"Okay, I'll take the hint. But he is cute, and he looks hungry."

Many people left the kitchen while the pair were eating, but the pup was still at his post when they stepped out. "I don't care who his master is, I'm getting him something to eat," grated Julie. She popped in and emerged with a side order of bacon and some scraps she'd begged from the luncheon carving board. The little beast wagged his appreciation, buried his face in the paper plate of goodies, began to inhale greedily. He lifted his head long enough to look after her once, but made no move to follow her as she walked away.

"See, he is waiting for somebody," said Monty as they rounded the corner.

"Somebody that doesn't feed him much! If he's still there tomorrow, I'm taking him home," she said flatly.

Monty nodded. He had finally learned not to agrue

with Julie when she was engaged in championing the un-
derpuppy.

It did not take Bonnie long to readjust to the life of
the racetrack, and soon she was walking quietly beside
Moriarty to and from the course with hardly a glance at
the milieu.

For three days Monty persuaded Julie to leave the little black pup beside the kitchen, his permanent post; but
when he appeared in their path on Saturday morning,
Julie scooped him up and carried him back to the tack
room.

"Fellas, I'd like you to meet Percy," she called happily down the shed. The dog wagged all over and rolled
onto his back, delighted to be the center of attention. "I
haven't got the shelter begun yet, but that doesn't mean
I can't get started. I'll take him home until I can place
him. Isn't he a dear?"

"Fat chance that dog has of leaving, once he sets paw
on Deepwater Farm," Monty mumbled, unheard.

Beau had the same idea. "Li'l boy, you really lucked
out; you got a home for life."

Julie looked at them suspiciously. "You're not thinking that I'm going to keep him? For good? Why—well
—oh, I guess he would be nice for keeping Barney company."

"Who's Barney?"

"A wolfhound pup that Monty and I rescued. He was
so hurt . . . the cast should come off his leg in two
weeks, but he'll have to take it easy for a while, and if
he has Percy here to lie around with and talk to—I
mean, Pushy has Nana, so it's only fair. But when the
shelter's finished and we have all sorts of nice people
looking for dogs, if the right folks come along for this
puppy, he'll go home with them! I *mean* it, Monty! The
shelter's not a way to build up a big kennel of mixed

canines for *me*, it's to find real homes for good animals. And I'll have a lot of fun matching them up."

"Julie," Monty said soberly, "aren't you a little premature, counting on your shelter? I know how important it is to you, but you're financing the project in your mind with Bonnie's winnings and she hasn't won them yet. Nobody can predict the outcome of *any* race. You of all people must know there's no such thing as a sure winner in racing."

"Bonnie's going to win!" she flared at him.

"You can't be certain of that, and it's unhealthy to think in such a crazy way!" Having finally flared out at *her*, Monty's desperation to make the girl see reason carried him on. "Try to be realistic, will you! Bonnie's an outstanding horse, sure. Nobody will ever take that away from her. But she's been away from the races for more than two years. She's had a serious fracture, dropped a set of twins, and is now trying to make it back. I grant you—shut up a minute!—she's training very well right now. Better than ever. But she's older, much older for a Thoroughbred, and we have no guarantee that she's still the athlete she was! Even if she proves to be," he finished, spluttering a little with earnestness, "we don't *know* she can win against horses who've been running steadily, and are two or three years younger than she is!"

"If she runs, she'll win," said Julie quietly, calmly. "I'm certain of it. If she doesn't, that's the breaks of the game; I could take it. But it won't happen that way. She'll win, because she's Bonnie."

Even Monty could see that there was no sense in pursuing an argument when he was dealing in apples and Julie in oranges; with a growl, something to do with "illogical conviction," and a shrug and a sigh, he retreated.

When morning chores were finished, it was nearly

eleven. In the silence that would prevail till the calling of the first race, Julie departed for Deepwater, the little black puppy tucked under her arm.

Mirror Image, a lean roan two-year-old Deepwater colt, was slated to make his racing debut in the seventh race. So, after a light lunch in the track kitchen, Monty headed for the tack room with the racing paper to study the past performances of the competition and wait out the hours till the horses were called to the paddock. At the barn he found Drop Cord sitting in front of the colt's stall, absently rolling bandages.

"What d'you think, Drop Cord? We have a shot?"

The head groom smiled, squinting up at Monty from beneath the brim of his soft wool cap. "If this colt breaks good, 's'only one horse he's got to beat: that chestnut of Wilson Cain's. Course, anything can happen once they leave that gate, but if he's anywhere close at the head of the lane, I think he can take it all."

"Optimism's a wonderful thing, and I'm surrounded with it," said Monty. "But it can foster some crushing disappointments. Look at Julie. She believes that Bonnie's unbeatable. You've seen how she's building her hopes for the animal shelter around that premise. No horse is invincible."

"Right."

"But I think it'll tear her apart if the mare gets beat. Break her heart. Hang it, I almost wish we'd hadn't tried to bring Bonnie back!"

"Miss Julie is a fine, fine person," said Drop Cord slowly, "and I'd purely hate to see her disappointed that bad. I haven't had the pleasure of knowin' her as long as the rest of you folks, but if she's countin' that heavy on her mare, then Bonnie'll just have to win, won't she?"

"You're as superstitiously unreasonable as Julie," said Monty, exasperated. "Hasn't it occurred to anyone under this shed that maybe she *can't* win every time they ring the bell? Man alive, there could be something out there that's faster than Bonnie! Or maybe it'll rain: she's not overly fond of mud. Or maybe she'll get boxed in, or stumble, or have to go the long way round. Or maybe I'm only supposed to run her when I've been told by some oracle that she can't lose! Like for a $5,000 claiming tag!"

"Your temperature's rising, boss. I only meant that we'd do everything possible to put the odds in her favor. The rest, that's up to Bonnie and Beau, and they're the last ones in this world to let your little lady down."

"She's not my little lady," grunted Monty, seeing a taunt where none had been intended.

"Yes she is. Now if you'll keep an eye on this colt for me, I'll trot down for a sandwich before the kitchen closes."

"Go ahead, Drop Cord. It's a long while till post time." Monty watched the big man disappear around the corner, then ambled toward the tack room, pausing briefly outside Bonnie's stall. "Guess I've turned into a spoilsport, Bonnet baby," he said to her glumly. *"You* know, anyway, that winning stakes races isn't quite so easy as some people think." He scratched her ear. "Julie's counting on you—too heavily—so you, well, you just do the best you can." He went on, shaking his head. "She's got *me* talking to animals," he muttered.

Chapter FOUR

Morning comes early to the backstretch. Sleepy-eyed grooms, snatched rudely from bed by the clock, fumble with buttons and grope for shoes in the dark, unwilling to finish the night till they must. In silence they step out into four-o'clock blackness, moving mechanically along the rows of stalls.

They pause outside the stalls, hands feeling along the walls to locate switches, and in the sudden blaze of light squint sidelong at the occupants. Soft brown eyes, caught with pupils wide in full night vision, blink back at them with mild accusation.

Aroused by light, the horses stretch and yawn, walk around, or scramble to their feet in graceful-ungainly fashion, shaking free the straw that clings to their manes and tails. Slowly they join the day, moving cautiously to the doors, thrusting their heads into the aisles with ears twitching lazily. A groom with key in hand unlocks the feed-room door, and like an army drill team every long head turns smartly toward the sound. He rolls the grain cart down the shed, doling out the morning ration and setting in the tubs, which have been removed from the stalls overnight, with practiced ease. The horses at the farthest point stamp and whinny with impatience. When the last horse has been fed, quiet descends once more, broken only by the rhythmic purling undertone of munching jaws and grinding teeth.

Most of the grooms will have let their charges eat in peace, grasping the opportunity to hastily visit the track kitchen, or perhaps to plug in the coffee pot in their tack room. Within half an hour the horses will have finished eating and the sky will begin to lighten. Within the hour the track will open, and the first of a host of Thoroughbreds—at least six hundred, perhaps as many as two thousand five hundred—will set hoof upon the carefully manicured surface.

Beginning a day when it's only four hours old is seldom anyone's idea of fun. It is a matter of necessity. When a track offers an afternoon program of racing, the first race is generally scheduled to go off at one or one thirty. The surface of the track must be in the finest condition that the weather permits. This means that the maintenance crew must have time to repair the morning damage, working with harrows, drags, floats, sprinklers. (In the winter, they have been known to run the harrows throughout the night to prevent the track from freezing!)

So the training hours begin with dawnlight: five thirty or so; and usually end at ten or ten thirty, with a quarter-hour break at eight for a quick trip around with the harrow. If a trainer with more than a couple of horses in his stable is to be assured of getting them all to the track within the time limit, giving each beast the necessary attention while working and cooling out, and still allowing for the usual delays, occasional mishaps, and rare emergencies, the men who help him must start early. Even if everything could be counted on to go smoothly (which it cannot), horses should have an hour in which to digest their feed before they are asked to perform any physical activity.

Kandahar Park was no different from other race-tracks across the country. In the Deepwater stable, however, there was one pleasant variation on the routine: Drop Cord, the head groom, always took it upon himself to mix the feed in the afternoon and to feed the entire stable complement in the morning. The other grooms were grateful to him for their extra minutes of sleep, and were quick to volunteer for chores during the day to express their appreciation. Drop Cord always waved away their thanks with a smile, insisting that "It's *my* time o' day," and "I like to get up and meet the day head-on and kind of solitary."

Monty habitually appeared at five, checked briefly with Drop Cord on the condition of each horse, and retired to the tack room to drink coffee and mark the chart for the morning's work. Dan Gibson, his assistant trainer, arrived on his heels, bringing their three regular exercise boys with him in his one-driver car pool. The hot-walkers could be counted on to be there by six, which was generally just in time to catch the first set as they returned from the track. Julie had horses to work at the farm, but with careful timing managed to reach the track a few minutes before eight. Monty scheduled the horses so that Bonnie would go to the track as soon as it reopened after the harrow-break, to take advantage of the freshly leveled dirt; but the big mare never left the shed without Julie and the pony Moriarty.

Now Monty sipped his coffee, absently eyeing the date on the morning edition of the *Racing News*. Sixteen days until the Marquesa, and Bonnie couldn't have been better. He shifted his gaze to the training chart listing all his horses, and the penciled figures across from Bonnie's name in last Monday's square, which noted the time and distance of her latest work.

Drop Cord's big lanky frame loomed in the doorway, then crossed to the trunk in the back corner. Lifting the tray, he reached down into the depths and brought out a dark blue blinker hood with small leather cups sewn to the outer edges of the eyeholes. "Dan said you want to try cheaters 'stead of half cups or cutouts on Charter Flight today. Have to use the new ones; Ace Saddlery hasn't repaired the old ones yet."

"Fine with me," said Monty. "He can't gallop without blinkers, he's all over the racetrack; but he won't break from the gate with 'em. I think the cheaters may be a compromise on both counts. Marsh can take him once around easy, then go to the gate."

As Drop Cord stepped out into the shed, a slim figure rounded the corner and a small hand tapped his elbow. "Excuse me," a very hesitant voice began, "are you Mr. Drop Cord?"

The groom looked down at a boy with light brown hair and serious gray eyes, who stood fifteen inches short of his own six-foot-five. The slender frame was deceiving; the boy was at least sixteen, perhaps a little older. But sober innocence radiated from him.

"My name is Cheney, but I *am* called Drop Cord by my friends, yes. You're new around here, right? What can I do for you?"

"I work for Foster Garnett—that is, I just began working for him not long ago; this is my first day, actually," said the boy in a rush. "I'm going to be a jockey, but first I have to learn about the racetrack. Mr. Garnett he sent me to Justin Wells in Barn 3 to pick up a saddle-stretcher and the key to the quarter pole. He's in a terrible hurry for them because he wants to work a horse this morning; but Mr. Wells said he gave them to Tommy Tate in Barn 26, and *he* said Katherine Lyle borrowed them from him. She's in Barn 48, clear on the other side, but by the time I got there, she'd given them to David Hansen in seventeen. He wasn't there, but his foreman said I should see if you have 'em because he handed them over to Mr. Everett, whoever he is."

"I heard of Mr. Everett someplace, sure," said Drop Cord. He winked at Monty, who refused to meet his eye. With a note of sincere regret he told the lad that he was terribly sorry, but he'd had both items in his hands not ten minutes before. Here he spread those hands out before the boy's face; they were so enormous that the poor fellow started backward with astonishment. "Fact is, I just this minute came back from Norman Saville's stable, where I delivered both them things at the direction of old what'sisname, Mr. Everett. If only I'd known you were on the way, maybe Mr. Saville coulda waited till Mr. Garnett was finished with them."

"Well, I seem to be getting closer, anyway," said the boy with a sigh. "If you'd tell me the way to Mr. Saville's barn, I better get moving. Mr. Garnett is going to fire me sure before I even finish my first day, at this rate."

Drop Cord nodded, and somberly informed him that Norman Saville was stabled in Barn 40. "Last barn on this side. His colors are gray and gold. You can't miss it. Ask for Chip Dawson, he's in charge over there." The boy turned to leave. "Tell him I sent you," added Drop Cord helpfully, as the other vanished at a dogtrot.

The groom contained himself for a moment, then burst into deep chuckles. Monty shook his head. "The oldest gag on the track," he said, "and they still fall for it. I'll bet that they were sending green kids for things like that two hundred and fifty years ago, in the days of the Byerly Turk and the Godolphin Arabian. If everybody's as helpful as you are, that boy 'll run his legs off before he realizes that it's racetrack humor."

"You know old man Garnett," said Drop Cord. "Done it with every last one of his boys. Makes riders

out of 'em, too, in the long run; but always has his
laugh at their expense. He says, if they come up grinning, and can laugh at themselves, then they're worth his
time and trouble."

"I'd almost forgotten that's how you got your name.
What was it that you were sent after? Don't tell me that
Garnett was the man."

"A drop cord and a pair of left-handed reins. And it
was the same Garnett. I just turned fourteen, it was my
first summer at the track. The old man—well, he wasn't
so old then—used to divide his time between New York
and Florida accordin' to season. I wasn't so tall then,
and I had dreams of riding races. Garnett, he started me
on that goose-pursuit, and somebody along the line even
gave me a cord, just to keep it interesting. Man!" said
Drop Cord, smiling in reminiscence, "I walked and ran
and finally staggered more'n ten mile that day. All over
Belmont Park! Finally saw how foolish I'd been, and it
was all I could do not to blubber. But I brought him
the cord anyhow, and managed a grin, and he gave me
my name on the spot. It stuck, and I forgot how far I'd
gone to earn it." He cocked his head, remembering his
first years on the racetrack. "I stuck with the old man,
too, till I got too big to ride. Then I went to workin' for
Doc Lejeune. He always called me Cheney, but when I
came back to the track it was Drop Cord again. It feels
more like me, you know?"

"It's a wonder that no one ever sent Julie on the
tour," said Monty, thinking out loud. "What a perfect
candidate she'd have made, when she was green and eager——"

"Take a pretty mean dog to pull that stunt on her,"
Drop Cord said, interrupting him. "She's so sure that
this rough old world is a wonderful place to live in, and
that the people are all so good . . . "

"Minus a few notable exceptions," said Monty, "such

as Alex Homer and Zeke Matthews the horsenappers,[1] and Earl Mariner the horse-whipper,[2] and Robert Lenkes and Nicholas Grey the record-fakers,[3] and Alexis Markham[4] who did her best to kill Julie . . . aside from those, yes, she trusts the whole wide world."

"Well, I for one 'ld do anything you could name to keep her good world intact," said Drop Cord darkly. "If I could, I'd cast me a magic spell on Bonnie there, and make sure she got her trip to the winner's circle after the running o' the Marquesa!"

"If you need any help on that, O mighty sorcerer, count me in as an up-and-comin' accomplice!" Beau Watkins, the jockey, had joined them in the tack room. "Fact is, I may try a little bit of witchery out there myself on May third," he said, rubbing his hands together in a gesture of pure wickedness. "Gonna read up on voodoo, hoodoo, and you-do! Not that we'll need it, but some magic, black or white or pale blue, can't hurt. 'Sides, Bonnie and Julie are due for some smooth sailing. Had enough trouble to last them a lifetime or two. Between crooks and frauds and crazies, broken bones and horsethieves, to not even *mention* the ghosts and the twins—" he caught himself in midsentence. "Why don't I step down off this soapbox and get to gallopin' horses?" He started out the door, turned back. "Don't you alarmists worry about the Marquesa. It's as good's in the bag. Just think of how you'll spend your stake, Drop old boy; I'm set to buy some real estate with mine."

Even Monty had to laugh. If the owner, the groom, and the jockey could be so idiotically confident of winning a race that was sixteen days off, who was the trainer to argue in the cause of reason?

1. *The Sweet Running Filly*
2. *A Horse Called Bonnie*
3. *Sunbonnet: Filly of the Year*
4. *Bonnie and the Haunted Farm*

It was barely seven o'clock when Julie appeared at the barn, explaining that Doc Haffner was scheduled to worm the entire farm that day and therefore no horses were to be worked. She went directly to Bonnie's stall, intending to surprise the good mare by her early arrival, but the horse would not be caught off-guard and snuffled a throaty welcome at the first sound of Julie's stride on the hard-packed clay of the shed. After a short visit with the outstanding star of Deepwater Farm, Julie took one turn around the shed to find and exchange a few words with each member of the stable crew.

Julie saw nothing unusual in this daily pattern she set for herself, and was oblivious to the fierce loyalty she inspired in every man of them. Racetrackers are, by and large, a cynical group, used to the whims of chance, the shifting luck of the game, the various levels of their society that are as strictly kept as the ancient Hindu caste system. Rarely does a person of Julie's stature, an owner of one of the best stakes mares in the world, treat the "hands" as equals; never as friends. Yet it did not occur to Julie to do otherwise. So, as Beau had said to Monty that first time when Bonnie won for him, "We had to win for Julie. She gives so much more than most people that you want to give her back something really fine. I hope she never learns just how mean and cruel this business can be. I hope she never finds out that folks aren't as great as she thinks. Let her believe in the horses! They may let her down once in a while, but not for the lack of tryin'." That summed up quite well just what Julie did to people.

Her morning rounds completed, Julie hurried to join Monty and Dan as they headed to the trainers' stand to watch the next set gallop. She always delighted in the atmosphere of the track as intensely as did Bonnie. The familiar routine in the stable area, the endless wave of Thoroughbreds in motion on the track in the morning hours, and the unmatchable thrill of tension, speed, and high emotion when they met and clashed, won or lost in the strenuous trials of the afternoon. It all came alive for her each time she entered the gates. There were other exciting ways of life, but hers was racing and she loved it. She knew, too, that no matter how many horses she met, schooled, trained, rode, petted and cared for and loved in the course of her lifetime, in the end there would still be only one horse that had it all, that meant everything: Sunbonnet.

When she had seen everyone, Julie returned to the shed to set the tack on Bonnie and get Moriarty, the pony, ready so that he and she could accompany Bonnie and Beau. As usual, Drop Cord had the bay hide gleaming; it would have been simple for him to go ahead and tack the mare himself, but he always left this ritual to Julie.

Spread the saddle cloth over the shiny back, put the pad on top and fold the cloth over. Now set the saddle carefully in place, secure the girth. Take the horse's front legs one by one and pull them out in front of her to smooth any folds of skin that might pinch beneath the girth. Tighten this another hole or two. So much for the saddle. Reins over the neck, bit eased into the horse's mouth, crown piece slid gently over the ears and the throat latch buckled: that about takes care of the bridle. Check to see that the browband lies straight and is neither too high nor too low.

While Julie tacked Bonnie, Drop Cord readied Moriarty and let him across the shed to wait outside for Julie. Leaving the patient pony ground-tied with his reins trailing, he stepped back into the aisle in time to give Beau a leg up onto the back of the beautiful mare. Julie mounted Moriarty and met Beau and Bonnie at the end of the shed. Together they walked to the gap, arriving as the entrance barrier was lifted.

"That's what I call timing," said Julie, as they started onto the track. "We're leaving our hoofprints where no horse has trod before."

"Not for long," said Beau, eyeing two sets of three and at least five single riders about to converge on the same spot.

They turned their horses the wrong way of the track, the placid pony jogging to keep up with the dancing mare. They reversed direction at the quarter pole and struck out at a smart trot. Moriarty's short legs were no match for the engulfing strides of the Thoroughbred, and he swiftly resorted to a canter in an effort to stay with Bonnie. They passed the gap and continued to the wire, where Julie eased the pony to the outside rail as Beau let Bonnie break into a gallop.

"Meet you as usual," Beau called over his shoulder as the big mare settled into the serious work of conditioning.

Julie walked the pony to the first turn, and stood him facing the infield with his tail against the outside rail. There she would wait until Bonnie had gone the required distance, after which Beau would pull up and rejoin her. She stood in her irons and twisted around so that she could see the trainers' stand. Finding Monty among several men standing there, she waved gaily, then focused her attention on Sunbonnet.

As always, she was aware of shivers, even gooseflesh, as she watched the magically fluid motion of her horse. The powerful hindquarters that rose and fell, driving her forward with what seemed effortless ease, would never cease to amaze Julie. How could one horse have so much? Speed, power, endurance, a will to win that would not let her give up—was there ever before such a horse as she? (Julie knew perfectly well that there had been quite a number, since the early eighteenth-century days when the three great foundation sires of the Thoroughbred breed were alive. From Alsab to Citation, from Man o' War to Gallorette there had been many all-but-perfect horses down the years. But they hadn't belonged to Julie Jefferson!)

What might Bonnie have been, though, if the injury hadn't stopped her in midcareer? And now look at her. How could anyone doubt that she would win? All anyone had to do was *look*.

Julie's total preoccupation with Bonnie's every movement on the track was nothing new. The undying thrill of watching the magnificent animal had always absorbed her mind completely. So concentrated was her attention, so intensely did she feel akin to the pounding hoofs, the sweeping stride, the urge to fly, that she was unaware of what was happening near the gap.

She never saw the big black two-year-old bearing out around the turn at the eighth pole. She didn't know it when he suddenly bolted toward the gap in a frantic, mindless effort to leave the track. She paid no notice to the outrider who spurred his horse into action and prevented the black colt from getting out, but failed to catch him as he pelted by. She was so wrapped up in Bonnie that she at first ignored the racket of the exercise boy bawling, shrieking, cursing: "Heads up! Look out! *Outrider!*" as the terrified horse surged out of control, heading straight for the outside rail. The outrider saw the danger and screamed a warning too, but his words were lost in the wind and the commonplace hubbub of the track.

At last, as the sounds penetrated her absorption, Julie looked away from Bonnie. Too late, she saw the impending collision and tried desperately to rein Moriarty out of the path of the fear-crazed colt. She was not fast enough. The full force of a twelve-hundred-pound Thoroughbred traveling at forty miles an hour smashed headlong into Moriarty.

The big colt rammed the startled pony broadside, catching him full behind the shoulder. The dreadful impact of the abrupt stop sent the exercise boy sailing thirty feet up the track, while both horses and Julie crumpled together and went to the ground in a horrible chaos of tangled legs, leather, bodies. . . .

There was no way of escape for Julie as she was hurled face down into the dirt, buried beneath flailing legs, twisting barrels, and cleated feet. She could only lie there as the beasts scrambled and thrashed, unable to avoid the great black hoof that smashed heavily down on her back.

Chapter *FIVE*

From his vantage point on the trainers' stand, Monty Everett saw the black horse bolt to the outside. He watched with grim fascination as the outrider's stout brown pony was distanced in a few strides; then realized with a rush of horror that the frenzied black was running on a collision course, holding a straight and certain line that ended with the jaunty little patchwork pony and— Julie.

His Julie! "Julie! Julie, watch out!" The sound of his voice was like some stranger's to him, thin and faraway. *"Julie!"* he fairly screamed her name. He must race down to her, snatch her safe from the onslaught of those terrible hoofs, but in no way could he get there in time. Fear twisted his belly, filled his legs with lead. "Julie!" The word died on his lips, he knew she could not hear him. Some way to warn her, there must be a way. . . . Couldn't she hear the rider shrieking and swearing as the runaway gathered speed?

"Dear God, *make* her hear!"

And the outrider, too. Couldn't she hear one or the other? Monty could hear them clear over here! "Make her see! Make her hear! Don't let them hit her!" He was shouting, the other trainers on the stand were roaring too. But they were much farther from Julie than the black colt.

Monty saw her head jerk round, could almost hear her gasp as she took in the situation. He prayed ferociously, instantaneously, that she could move Moriarty in time, in the same instant that he recognized the utter lack of all time now. Terror iced him, forced his unwilling eyes to watch as the three bodies smashed together, twisted, crumpled, fell writhing in a grotesque nightmare dance figure. . . .

Then Monty could move. With a leap he went from the stand to earth, almost before the two thrashing horses had fallen he had vaulted over the railing. Somewhere under a ton of panicky horseflesh lay his girl. His only girl. Three-eighths of a mile seemed an endless road as he ran. He would never arrive, he would be running forever. How far had he come? Where was Julie, why couldn't he see her? Was no one in Kandahar Park but Monty Everett going to her aid?

The black colt scrambled to his feet, eye-whites popping, mouth gaped; the reins flying about his head and stirrups whipping sharply at his sides, he took up his mad devil's race again.

Monty's lungs were bursting, but he did not know it. The painted pony stumbled somehow to his feet; scared mindless by the violent, unforeseen assault, it took poor Moriarty some long seconds to regain his balance. Then he was aware of a searing pain in his left shoulder. As he hobbled forward to escape the agony, dragging his almost useless foreleg, Monty covered the last of his run and caught a first glimpse of Julie.

He flung himself down beside her twisted, dirt-spattered form, reaching for her hand. He dared not touch her otherwise, for she was plainly hurt badly and must not be moved by an amateur attempts at first aid. He stared into her bloodless, chalky face, and her eyes opened, unfocused, to stare at him. Monty gave chaotic mental thanks for the well-made Caliente Safety Helmet and the universal racetrack mandate that required it to be worn.

An outrider had summoned the ambulance, while another stood by the inert girl, sending on their way the curious exercise boys on their horses, the assorted railbirds, everyone, in short, but Monty. "Room for the ambulance, you knuckleheads! Keep clear!"

She was so helpless lying there in the rag-doll limpness, unable to move from her strange and unnatural posture; Monty yearned to give her reassuring words, comforting words, but he could not force his voice past the constriction of his throat. Was that unendurable pain in her blue eyes? Tears had already streaked the smudged dirt on her cheeks. The hand he held was cold and very clammy.

Actually, Julie was unaware of pain, and only knew that she was suffused with a kind of chill dizziness, a vertigo in which things spun slowly round her and would not rest. She was faint, could feel the waves of giddy weakness come and go beyond her control.

"Don't move, baby. The ambulance is pulling up now," said Monty, angry at his stupidity—was *that* all he had to say to her? "Lie quiet, honey. I love you. You'll be all right. I love you too much for . . ."

Even he had no idea what he had been about to promise her.

Sweat and tears stood out on great drops on her face, glistening against the dark smears and the sheet-pale skin. She clutched convulsively at his fingers. *Don't move*, he said.

She could not have moved if he'd told her to.

Julie Jefferson could not stir.

The ambulance men pounced out of their seats, opened

the doors, slung out the stretcher and blankets with eco-
nomical motions.

"I said to clear out of the way, you meat-head blath-
erskites!" snarled the guardian outrider at a couple of
well-meaning trainers who had come over to offer their
help.

Then Beau trotted up on Bonnie, and Monty, lifting
his head, said, "Beau," flatly, and stood up from Julie's
side, his face nearly as pale as hers.

The jockey had seen that there'd been an accident,
and to keep Bonnie as far as possible from the commo-
tion had delayed turning her back and kept her walking
on the far side of the track. Finally, when he'd decided
that he couldn't wait any longer to take her in, he had
turned back on the rail, intending to pass the scene of
the mishap as swiftly as possible. Only when he'd actually drawn alongside the group did he realize that it was
his beloved Julie who had been hurt. He slid from the
saddle and, leading the startled mare by the reins, shoved
past the protesting outrider toward Monty.

"What happened, boss?"

"Look," said Monty in a voice that neither of them
recognized, "look, Beau, take Bonnie to the shed." He
gripped him by the arm for the comforting of them both.
"Tell Drop Cord to—I don't know—to do as he sees
fit."

"Hang in there, boss," said Beau, clamping his fingers
on Monty's arm in his turn. "Is Julie—"

"She'll be just fine. What was . . . oh, tell Drop
Cord that Bonnie can stand in fours. And you get the
vet, *fast*, for Moriarty. Yes. I don't know where he is."

Beau glanced around. "Down yonder with somebody."

"Hurry it up," said Monty, "tell Dan to finish the
horses. I'll call you. Later, yes, later. When I know. Go
on, old fella."

"You hang tough, hear?" demanded Beau, almost crying with the fear and ignorance of what the full state of affairs might be. Don't worry 'bout us." He turned away, wrestling slightly with a Bonnie who wanted to go to her girl.

Julie gasped, and Monty was kneeling beside her. "My legs," she said huskily. "Monty, where are my legs?"

Then the two ambulance attendants were firmly pushing him aside. They spread a canvas lift sheet beside Julie, gently lifted her and laid her on it, hoisted sheet and girl onto the stretcher; carried this to the ambulance and slid it in over the rollers.

They did not turn on their siren until they were far enough from the track not to frighten any of the valuable, hypersensitive racehorses.

As Monty ran for his own car, Beau led Bonnie back to the Deepwater barn and sadly reported the news, or what small part of it he knew, to Drop Cord and the others. All he could actually say for sure was that Julie looked awful. "I don't know, man," he kept telling them as they questioned him furiously, "I just don't know!" He relayed Monty's orders for the horses. "Maybe we find out more when Moriarty gets here. That outrider, the good one, what's his doggone name? Steve Rush, he caught Mori down the track. Scorchy, you get the vet on the phone, get him here fast if he isn't coming already. I got to do all the thinking here? Move!"

"Nobody said Mori was hurt," Drop Cord told him firmly.

"I got to say everything?" shouted Beau. "He's hurt!"

Drop Cord laid a huge and soothing hand on the boy's shoulder. "Take it easy, Watkins, or you'll pop all your blood vessels. What we need least around here is a nervous-brokedown jockey."

"Right. Sorry. It's Julie. I know her since she was a

little kid. I'd *die* for that girl," said Beau, crying at last.
"I'd die."

"No need. Sit down and smoke a cigarette and—"

"You know I don't smoke!"

"Sit down, anyway, before you keel over."

"Stash Watkins never raised his kids to keel over,"
said Beau, and collapsed on a bale of straw.

Moriarty appeared shortly, led by Steve Rush, who
told them about the black colt as he helped with the laboring pony. Moriarty lurched into his stall, the stress of
his effort plain in his heavy breathing and the sweat that
streamed from his body and collected in little puddles beneath his belly. His large white patches, so snowy and
clean a quarter of an hour before, were stained with dirt
and muddied by his sweat. His nostrils flared scarlet, his
head hung low. The gentle, loving eyes were glazed with
fear and agony.

Drop Cord talked steadily and calmly as he assessed
the damage. The rest of the Deepwater crew were clus-
tered around the outrider, asking questions, vocally
chewing over the calamity and its possible results.

"I don't know what set the black off, or why she
didn't see him coming," Steve said. "Except for a few
cuts and bruises, that colt looked all right to me when he
went snorting past after the smash-up. His boy, somebody told me, banged up his head and broke his collar-
bone. He was able to walk back to his barn, so I guess
there wasn't anything worse happened to him. Funny
thing is, I don't believe he had any idea that Miss Jefferson was hurt. He just went straight to his barn, and
that's on the other side of the track."

"Crack on the head addles a man," said Drop Cord
from the stall behind them. "So does a runaway. No
blame to the kid."

"I don't guess he meant to be run off with like that,"
said Beau judiciously, having recovered some of his own

equilibrium. "When a horse bolts, it's—it's like a big light goes on in his head and blinds him, and I don't care who you are, you won't stop him till *he* gets ready to quit. Don't help Julie any, no matter how or why he came to slam into her."

Drop Cord set several of his boys to the task of rubbing Moriarty dry. Obviously he couldn't be walked, for it had been all he could manage to make it to his stall; so scraping and toweling would have to suffice.

While they worked on the injured pony, Beau and Drop Cord himself curried and brushed Bonnie, rubbed her legs with liniment and rolled on neat flannel bandages. Neither could turn his thoughts from the good little person who owned this mare and loved her above everything else. The confident, courageous girl who always walked in sunlight whatever the weather, who gave so much to others . . . who was herself a gift . . . now lay in some hospital bed, hurt—no one could tell them how badly. There was absolutely nothing they could do for her, beyond taking their usual perfect care of her fine horse. This helplessness overwhelmed them both. At last Beau straightened and said, "You know what we got to do, man?"

"What *can* a couple of horse people do?" asked Drop Cord without expecting an answer. Then he stared into Beau's eyes, and they nodded and said it almost simultaneously.

"With Julie out of action, we got to see that this mare *wins!*"

Solemnly they shook hands.

A track veterinarian after a careful examination found that, aside from some minor scrapes, the only harm done to Moriarty was a badly torn muscle in his left shoulder. However, that was enough. It would be a long time healing, he told the silently waiting men, and his recommendation was that the pony be sent to the farm to recuperate.

"Poor old boy," said Beau, "what a miserable way to earn a vacation."

For the time being, he would be treated with pain-killers and anti-inflammatory agents, but after a reasonable period of this treatment, time would be the only possible healer.

Drop Cord patted the pony and offered him a carrot, which Moriarty ignored. "Looks like you'll always have a dent in that shoulder," he said. "Just hope the tissues mend strong enough so's you can use it all right."

When the vet had dispensed the necessary drugs and left them, the men of the shed row gradually returned to their normal work, though hushed or silent in an atmosphere of thickening gloom.

Despite the furor and delays caused by the accident, all the Deepwater horses made it to the track as scheduled, and by noon the routine chores were out of the way. The horses had been groomed to a fare-thee-well, perhaps out of a general sense of guilt at being so useless to Julie Jefferson; and those requiring bandages stood in meticulously wrapped two-and-fours, Bowie Mud had been packed in the feet that needed it. Sweats, leg paints, antiseptics, liniments had been applied to the appropriate limbs as directed. The midday grain ration had been dumped into the tubs, and the tubs hung in the stalls. The shed row had been raked smooth and watered to hold down the dust. Standing and running bandages, as well as the saddle cloths used in the morning, had been washed and hung up to dry on the clothesline stretched between two posts directly across from the tack room. Still, no one was inclined to leave, not even to make the short run to the kitchen for coffee or lunch, although it was well past racetrackers' mealtime. Nobody had much to say. Each of them knew that the others, too, were hovering on the edge of anger or despair, waiting for word of Julie's condition.

Drop Cord and the other three grooms were suddenly inspired to rearrange their wall boxes. This meant removing all the medicines, bandages, pins, tapes, tools, grooming utensils and multiple sundries that swiftly accumulate there in the cabinetlike "boxes" mounted on the walls. Then, after thoroughly cleaning the insides of the boxes and each item that would be returned, the things were all put back carefully . . . usually in the exact spot from which they had been taken. With care, this operation could be extended for the best part of an hour.

Dan Gibson and Beau busied themselves "reorganizing" the tack room: this included the absolutely indispensable unpacking and repacking of no less than four trunks, bulging at the seams with horse blankets, galloping boots, special reins and other devices for the control of problem horses; blinkers, coolers, fly sheets, halters, and much more. Spare bridles and saddles and all kinds of leather goods were routinely cleaned and put back again, till the time when they would be needed.

Marsh rounded up several spades and rakes, and after declaring in a gruffly defensive manner that his project was long overdue, enlisted the help of the remainder of the crew—the other exercise boy and all three hotwalkers—in the tedious task of leveling the center of the shed, which was constantly beaten into a narrow path by daily hammering of eighty shod feet.

It was midafternoon when Monty at last came back from the hospital.

Deeply touched to find the entire crew still assembled, he made a mental note to tell Julie of their interest, their patent concern for her.

"Well," said Beau, who had known Monty the longest

and was an acknowledged close friend, "what about her?"

"Under the circumstances," the trainer began, "she could have been hurt a lot worse—"

"Man, she could have been killed," said Drop Cord quietly. "Now tell us."

"They've got her pretty well doped up," said Monty, blinking. "They'll keep her that way for at least forty-eight hours. She's in a lot of pain, you can imagine; but worse, she's absolutely terrified."

"Why?"

"Because she has no feeling in her legs."

There was a silence, and Drop Cord again asked, "Why?"

"She was kicked in the spine by one of the horses. It crushed two vertebrae, which are causing the pain."

"You mean her back's busted?" cried Beau.

"No, no, not that bad. Two of the vertebrae are smashed in—not broken, just badly misplaced—and that equals suffering in any man's language. But the X-rays haven't shown any reason for her to have lost sensation in the legs. I got this from an orthopedic resident; all the others would say was 'Miss Jefferson has sustained an incapacitating spinal injury and we cannot estimate the extent of the damage at this time.'"

"But she'll be okay," said Beau tentatively.

"I don't know. I don't know any more than I just told you." Monty wiped his face with a dank handkerchief. "I called Julie's father in Ohio, and I'll meet him at the airport in the morning. Maybe they'll tell him more. Maybe they'll have found out more to tell him. I don't know."

The crew was stunned. They knew that Julie had been seriously hurt, and, being career racetrack men, they had no illusions about her rebounding with a gay smile from an accident as violent and savage as that caused by the black colt had been. They had imagined a multitude of cuts, an infinity of bruises, uncountable stitches, and broken bones without number. All of these, however, would mend. That she might have lost the use of her body was unthinkable; it had not occurred to any of them.

It was young Beau who broke the hush. "Not speaking for the others, but if there ever was time for a prayer to be said, I think it's now." He turned away and leaned his head against a post, his eyes shut.

"Beau's right," murmured Marsh, the exercise boy. "It's sure out of *our* hands now."

Monty glanced around the glum faces. Here was the harvest of the seeds that Julie Jefferson unknowingly planted every day of her life: he wondered whether the men would be embarrassed if he called it love.

They broke into groups, quietly drifting from the barn.

Dan Gibson went over the chart with Monty, filling in the data necessary for maintaining the schedule of exercising for the next few days. Monty would be in whenever he could manage it, but Dan would be in charge. When they reached Bonnie's name, Monty called to Drop Crod and Beau to join them.

"Beau, you keep her moving just as you have been, and don't let her overdo anything. Drop Cord, you watch her legs as if they were Steuben glass, and if there's so much as a hair out of place, don't fool around with anyone here, just call Doc Haffner at Deepwater and tell him to come on the double!"

"Sure. One question."

"Go ahead."

"What," asked Drop Cord plaintively, "is stoopin' glass?"

"Steuben. It's expensive and fragile and precious. Like Bonnie's legs." Sighing, he gazed into space. "You know something? With all the pain, and the mystery of her own legs, and medicine and everything, all that girl thinks about, cares about, is Bonnie. Bonnie, as usual. Bonnie, of course." A wraith of a smile touched his lips as Monty realized the complete accuracy of this statement. "First and last, Bonnie," he said.

Drop Cord laid one of his immense hands on Monty's shoulder. "You tell her that with my care and know-how, that mare will win and win easy. No matter what!"

"How good the care is don't matter, and you know it," said Beau. "In those last minutes out there, it's just the horse and the jock. So you give her a message from me too, Monty. Tell her that *Beau* says Bonnie'll win, and that's a promise."

"What's that line about 'if wishes were horses'?" Monty looked at one dark earnest face and then the other. "Bonnie has to win, we all know it. You're right. She has to win for Julie."

Chapter **SIX**

Now and then, at intervals whose length she could not guess, Julie would struggle to rouse herself from the unreal world into which she had been plunged by the medications and the suffering.

Underneath the phantoms which she saw, or dreamed, there was an icy sickness of pain that strove to overcome her, to make itself felt clearly; this never won out, and slowly diminished in force until it was hardly more than a dull gnawing, like a rotten tooth whose nerves had elongated into her spinal cord.

Thirty-six hours after the accident, Julie opened her eyes for the second or tenth or sixtieth time, kept them open this occasion, and found that her vision was clearing. White smears became wall and ceiling, advancing, receding, slowly firming into white plaster surfaces. A fuzzy outline much closer was a man leaning over the bed. It began to resemble her father.

Rand Jefferson was in Ohio, of course. Julie shut her eyes and felt them watering, and opened them slowly; and it was he. "Dad? Dad, is that you?" The sound she made grated in her inner ears like an echo of the long, noisy nightmares she had been experiencing.

A hand came down on hers. "It sure is, honey," said a warm voice, hushed after the long wait. "Don't try to comprehend everything at once. I'm here for a few months. No hurry about waking up."

She stared at him vacantly. There were silver cobwebs all through the corridors of her mind.

"They've decided to let you come up for air, baby."

"I've been here a lot of hours, I guess." The croak was her voice because she could feel it rasping her throat.

"A fair number. A day and a half. You had to rest after tangling with a runaway."

"Runaway." She lifted one arm slowly, then the other. "A black, it was. I remember." She touched her face, exploring it with wakening fingers, especially the forehead and left cheek. "I feel like a gargoyle! Like a lumpy piece of dough."

"You have turned some unusual shades," said Rand; denying the awfulness of her appearance would have violated the bond of truth that these two had always had between them. "Navy blue, black, lavender . . . but they're only bruises and slight cuts, Julie. You had a mild concussion, too, but these effects will all disappear without trace."

"Why does my back hurt so much?" The accident was coming clearer in her mind now, and the pain was intensifying. "It wasn't really a freight train that ran over me," she said huskily, "but it feels like it. It was only one horse."

"Two. Your pony was in there too."

"Moriarty. Is he all right?"

"Yes."

"My back—"

"Two crushed vertebrae account for that, darlin'," said her father. "Prognosis is good on that count too.

Although they say it'll take quite a while for them to mend completely." He paused for a moment or two, to see if she would continue; then he asked gently, "What about your legs, Julie? How do *they* feel?"

Her response was so long in coming that Rand almost decided that she'd slipped off into drugged sleep again, but finally she spoke. "I don't really know, Dad. They feel . . . funny. Tingling. As if my feet were asleep all the way up my legs. That's queer, isn't it?"

He stood a little straighter and let a sigh escape him. Then he really smiled for the first time. "I'm sure it feels 'queer,' kitten, but it's the best news I've heard yet!"

"What?" demanded Julie, in a ghost of her habitual chaffing tone at such responses. "You're jolly 'cause my legs are asleep? You can go back to Ohio, you unnatural parent!"

"Absolutely. Right after I explain. You see, one of those vertebrae was pressing on a nerve, and that's why your legs went numb so quickly out there on the track. The thing was lying, or caught, or whatever their technical term may be, at such a bad angle that the doctor didn't want to attempt an operation unless it was absolutely necessary. But if feeling hadn't started to return in a reasonable length of time, he'd have done it, so as not to risk the complete destruction of the nerve."

"Say that a little simpler, Dad. I'm not truly with it just yet."

"Well, your physician hoped that they'd been able to shift things enough to relieve the pressure. The tingling means that they were successful, as I understand it. So I think the worst has been avoided. Operations on backbones aren't a great deal of fun."

"Oh, I remember. You had one. For what Stash called a 'slippery disk.' But you came out fine," Julie said.

"And so would you, but it's nicer not to have an operation unless you truly must. Now the pressure ought to relieve itself, through immobilization, bed rest, and ultimately, physical therapy."

"Ultimately? How long are you talking about?"

"Don't know, dear."

"I've got to see Bonnie win the Marquesa!"

"If you're okay by then, you will, I'm sure."

"But I *have* to be!"

"All you have to do is get well. You can't set a time limit on that; not even the doctors can."

"But Dad!"

"Julie," he said seriously, holding her hand, "this particular time, you cannot go charging bullheaded and heedless into the situation, regardless of the consequences to yourself. You cannot make the rules. You cannot overcome obstacles with blind faith and determination. You have to lie quietly, follow orders, and be patient."

"But Bonnie will expect—"

"Julie."

"Yes, Dad?"

"You will promise me that you will do exactly, precisely, absolutely and only what the physician tells you to do."

"Yes, Dad."

"That's better." He smiled radiantly. "Sleep now, dear, your eyes look heavy. Monty will be here when you wake up in the morning."

Gratefully, Julie sank back into the cobwebbed corridors of her unconscious, and this time did not dream.

Next day, once in the morning and once in the afternoon, Julie was slid onto a cart, wheeled to the physical therapy room, slid onto the tilt table, and spent a quarter of an hour with her still-tingling feet propped against the baseboard and her body inclined at an angle of ten degrees. This was done so that when she was ready for a wheelchair, her circulation would not be so out of practice that it would knock her out if she sat upright. Each day the tilt table would be slanted a little farther from the horizontal.

Otherwise, treatment consisted mainly of lying as still as possible. After three or four days, the pain had quieted from excruciating to a dull, steady ache—uncomfortable, but not unbearable, or they would have operated.

As ordered by her specialist, the therapist then began to perform "passive exercises" during her time on the tilt table: moving her legs for her, slowly, not painfully, to maintain the muscle tone. In her own bed in the sunny, impersonal private room, she could lie supine or prone, or on either side, as long as she stayed straight. She was allowed to use her arms and turn her head, but not to twist her body; and after suffering one lacerating pang when she forgot her orders and reached for a glass of water, Julie was content to wait for the nurses or orderlies to come in every two hours and turn her. She grew stiff and sore, but the alternative was seizures of agony too sharp to bear.

Eventually the swellings disappeared from her face, although the dark splotchy patterns of bruises were visible for many days, and her torso kept a kind of spattered effect, like that of an Indian pony.

Rand or Monty was with her almost throughout each day's visiting hours—seven in the morning till eleven at night—and of course Monty had to deliver a daily account of Bonnie's training progress, as well as a general rundown of the entire string of horses at the track. As for other company, Rand Jefferson had a hard time keeping the visitors down to a figure that would not bring the charge nurse in on the double, brandishing her clipboard and demanding to know whether they all thought that Chambers Memorial was some sort of strange country club.

In addition to Monty's predictable arrivals, Rand knew he could expect that from two to eight employees of Deepwater or Fieldstone Farms would show up on any given day. The racetrack crew all made the journey at least twice, while Peaches, Scorchy, and the Deepwater group drifted in even more frequently. Peaches reported on the current status of Julie's canine corps (excellent), and once brought the good news that Barney's cast had been removed and the young wolfhound was robust and happy.

Leon, Stash, Pop, Doc Haffner, and the other Fieldstone cronies came down together, squashed and jammed into the usually adequate station wagon. When this small mob crushed into Julie's room, the charge nurse came clicking down the hall, starched within an inch of total rigidity, to scold the offenders. Pop took her into the hall and blarneyed her into a state of bewildered submission while Leon gave Julie the latest word on the twins and Tweedy and Cache, her gray jumper.

The next day brought Dirk Markham, Julie's friend from Croydon near Fieldstone, who carried two dozen roses and an exquisite antique music box covered with tiny, hand-carved horses.

Julie was surprised to see Dirk, and flushed with delight over the gifts. Monty shook hands with him heartily enough, but could not arrange his features into anything resembling great glee. Rand, whose passion as well as profession was antiques, recognized the quality of the music box, and wondered silently at the extravagence of it, till he had taken a good look at the light in the young man's eyes as he talked with Julie. Then Rand knew, and eyed Monty sideways and smiled ever so slightly. Competition! Maybe Mr. Everett would wake up now to the fact that life wasn't all horses. Or had he done so already, and was it Julie whose world was entirely equine? No, if Monty had ever proposed, Rand would have heard about it.

"How's old Cache?" asked Dirk, after the tale of the accident and news of Bonnie.

"The poor dear, he's riderless, and likely to stay that way for quite a while," said Julie sadly. Sometimes in the past month she had felt guilty about her big jumper, anyway, what with all the time spent on Bonnie. "He's going to forget everything we taught him, but I sure won't be able to work him for a while."

"I'll take him to Croydon tomorrow," said Dirk, patting her hand reassuringly. "Brisk him up a bit, and take him showing. That'll put a polish on him again. All right with you?"

"Oh, Dirk, that would be *so* good of you!" Julie reached up, and he bent forward for a hug. "Will you? It would be such a load off my mind."

"It's a promise."

"Nice fellow, that," said Rand when he'd left. "Very generous fellow. Like to see more of him."

"Oh, you will, Dad. He's a good friend, isn't he, Monty?"

"A good man," said Monty, rather gruff. "Had a lot of trouble recently, took it well. Good man with horses. He's okay."

"Handsome, too," said Rand, trying not to chuckle. "Mighty, mighty handsome."

The only absent face in those long weeks was that of Rollin Tolkov, Deepwater's owner, who was in Europe; but he called Julie every second evening to check on her progress and state of mind.

Because Julie had served notice on her doctor, as well as her father, Monty, the nurses, the physical therapist, and everyone who would listen, that she was going to the Marquesa if she had to go on a board, on her tenth

day in the hospital the physician strapped her into a spe-
cially constructed brace that would immobilize the injured section of her spine and had her put into a wheelchair. "Give you a few days to get used to this," he said.
"Take a roll down the hall with your father at the helm
two or three times a day. Then day after tomorrow we'll
have you take a few steps on the parallel bars."

Julie thanked him fervently, and rolled off in her
chair, trying to imagine that it would soon be a horse
under her again.

On the twelfth day, as promised, she was allowed a
chance at the parallel bars with the help of the physical
therapist. This, too, she managed—not easily or without
the ache becoming a pain, but without fainting or
screaming or even turning very pale. She was limited to
a few steps, and wasn't allowed to swing along the bars
as she'd anticipated—with her arms stiff, the therapist
on one side and an aide on the other holding and assist-
ing her, she moved jerkily and as though in slow motion,
placing very little weight on her feet. Then she was
helped into her wheelchair and pushed back to her room
by Rand.

"When will I be able to stand on my feet alone?" she
asked the doctor when he made his rounds.

"When I say so. Have to walk before we run, and
crawl before we walk."

"You're going to have me *crawl*—"

"It's an old saying," Rand put in. "I doubt that you
want her to creep around, sir?"

The doctor laughed briefly. "Heaven forbid. But I
think you'll be walking with crutches soon, Miss Jefferson. Shortly after you go home."

"Not by race day?" she said, dismayed.

"When's that?"

"May third."

"Oh no. Not that soon. I want you to have more rest, more therapy first."

"But I could stand now if you'd let me!"

"You won't need to stand to see your mare race. You'll be taken there by ambulance, the orderlies will put you in your chair, then you'll be brought back here as soon as it's over."

"I could stand," murmured Julie, rebellious after so much inactivity.

"Quite possibly. But not yet."

The next day she made a little more distance on the bars, and was allowed to sit in her wheelchair (complete with brace) while her father popped down to the cafeteria for lunch. Julie sat there feeling slightly achy and definitely defiant. She had no memory of promising her father to follow orders to the letter, for that first awakening had merged into her dreams and nightmares; she had been told several times afterward, until it stuck, just what had happened to her, but Rand had never thought to remind her of her solemn promise to obey the physician, because he had never realized that Julie had been talking under the influence of heavy sedation.

So she now rolled herself into what seemed a good position in relation to the bed, and cautiously forced her unwilling body to leave the chair and straighten itself upright.

Some of her confidence ebbed away. Her legs felt like warm jelly, and they wobbled more than she'd anticipated. She'd touched the floor with her feet while working on the parallel bars, but had not had her full weight on them since the accident. Easy does it. Stand here a minute. Then walk over to the bed and sit down, and show them that they're being too careful of you.

Right leg forward now. *Right leg forward.* Nothing happened. Why doesn't it do what it's told? she wondered, suddenly irritable with the stupid leg. All right: *left* leg forward. Move it. Come *on.*

Unable to support her weight any longer, or to propel her body toward the bed, Julie swayed and crumpled to the floor with a shrill, terrified scream.

When Rand came back some ten minutes later, he was greeted by a highly indignant charge nurse who began at once to lecture him and his daughter on foolish disobedience and disastrous consequences. Julie remained silent throughout the speech, lying in bed now with her face turned to the wall. When, as the nurse exited righteously and before Rand could ask what had prompted her to get out of the chair alone, the blond girl turned her head and showed her eyes running with tears.

"Dad—I can't stand on my legs, and I can't make them move!"

"Just what happened?" he asked steadily, his voice betraying none of the sudden dread he felt.

"They wouldn't hold me up. They just *melted,* Dad. And I tried to take a step but I hadn't any control. I tried, but I couldn't move."

"We'll talk to the doctor. The nurse is fetching him. Why did you try to walk, Julie?"

"I wanted to show that I could! I wanted to be on crutches at least, when Bonnie—"

"Don't you recollect what you promised me about obeying orders religiously?"

She stared blankly through the puddles of tears. "No."

"Okay, it was a rhetorical question. I knew you hadn't remembered the minute I heard about it. You were drugged. You'd never break a promise to your old man."

"Or to anybody, you know that! What did I say?"

They were still discussing this, Julie so amazed that she could have forgotten anything so important (medicine or no medicine) that she had all but forgotten her crash, when the physician came in looking stern. He examined her, and went off to order X-rays and tests, after being plainly dubious about her chances of going to the track.

Julie promised her father, without prompting this time, that she would always do precisely what the doctor ordered, even if it was to lie without budging for a month.

In the evening, while Monty was listening with ill-concealed horror to Julie's story, the doctor returned again. He sat down and looked at Julie for a moment in silence, while the girl gritted her teeth and Monty felt for the first time in his life as though he might faint. At last, "Well, you can go to your races," the elderly man said almost crossly. "If you follow your orders."

"She will," said Rand quietly. "What have you found out?"

"What I knew before. I was going to make those studies on her anyway—they're more sophisticated than the earlier ones, as a matter of fact they're dye studies, in which we inject dye into the spinal column and X-ray it —but I hadn't intended to do it quite yet. Her ambitious stroll today persuaded me to verify the matter."

"What's wrong with her?" said Monty in a voice that nobody recognized, least of all himself.

"An injury, but no pathological cause for the trouble. I use that term to mean 'no disease,' you understand. The vertebrae that were so rudely shoved in, my dear," he said to Julie, thawing a little at the tension in her face, "are putting pressure on a nerve. You can call it a pinched nerve, but I prefer the term 'pressured,' because that's all it is. A genuinely 'pinched' nerve might atrophy—waste away, die on you. Then you'd have real trouble. This is simply a nerve that's sustaining unnatural pressure."

"And?" Monty prodded.

"I decided after our preliminary findings to wait and see whether that pressure would respond to physical therapy, would gradually relieve itself. Anyone in the profession will tell you that I'm a conservative old cuss when it comes to operations, especially on the touchy area of the back. Well, you *are* responding."

"I am?"

"The two vertebrae have moved somewhat. I'm encouraged. I hope that the pressure will eventually be wholly released."

"Eventually. How long?"

"Nobody can say. Two months, three? I don't know. I can't prophesy. I may be wrong, and ultimately you may need that operation. But I hope not. Your progress so far is excellent."

"When I can't even stand alone, or walk?"

"You'll be walking soon with crutches. Your pain's a lot better, isn't it? You'll be able to keep it down with nothing more than aspirin. You'll follow my orders, do your therapy, and wait."

"I don't understand exactly why I'm not able to walk," said the girl sadly.

"The pressure on the nerve causes limited mobility," he said with great patience.

"What about manipulation?" asked Rand, whose knowledge of ailments was fairly extensive, though more in the animal world than the human.

"No, sir. Therapy, physical therapy alone, and the great healer itself."

"Time," nodded Rand.

"Time," said the physician solemnly.

"And I can see Bonnie race?" asked Julie, brightening. "If I'm a perfectly splendid patient?"

"You can see her race. Just don't get so excited that you try to stand up and cheer her to victory."

"What, Julie Jefferson?" said Monty. "Ridiculous!"

Chapter SEVEN

The morning of May third brought with it all the vitality and radiance of spring. The sun spilled brightly from a cloudless sky, splashing its warmth from the rocks and the ground, collecting in golden puddles that spread into giant pools extending for miles around. The sky was a rich, clear blue whose exact shade has no name, and a steady breeze gathered the fragrances of lilac, magnolia, and myriad wildflowers into a delicious riot of scent.

Monty Everett walked slowly down the shed in barn seven and paused for perhaps the twentieth time before the stall of the spectacular bay mare. He leaned heavily against the cut-out screen that was her door, resting his hands and chin in the U-shaped space that permitted the horse to poke her head out from behind the otherwise rectangular stall guard. Bonnie eyed him curiously. It was not unusual for him to stop by her stall; she was accustomed to find him there at any hour of the day or night. But today was different. It was barely ten o'clock in the morning and already he had appeared oftener than he did during any ordinary twenty-four hours.

He had stood outside the stall and stared at her. He had stepped inside and run his fingers down her legs, gently probing, testing, feeling for the slightest abnormality. He had met Drop Cord and Beau a hundred times coming and going in the shed, mumbling "Excuse me," and "I'm sorry," and "I didn't know I was in your way," as they moved about in the normal routine of preparing a horse to race.

Of course, the real conditioning had been accomplished in the months of carefully calculated exercise, designed to build physical fitness and stamina to a peak that would coincide with the running of a particular race. However, there are certain last-minute details that are little more than good horse sense, but are nonetheless essential.

There are such things as checking the position of the horse's shoes, making sure that they have neither shifted nor sprung and that the nails are firmly in place with the clinchers pinched down smoothly against the hoof. A raised clincher—the part of the nail that is cut off below the point after it has been driven into the hoof and is then bent over and rasped, partly to keep it from pulling loose and partly to protect the horse from cutting himself with it—can gash a horse's ankle, inflict a nasty puncture, or chop the opposing leg to ribbons as the horse drives himself forward at full speed. An injury like this, though frequently slight, can still render a horse lame for hours, days, or even upwards of a week; while at best he is unable to perform at his optimum when favoring an injured limb. Loose or shifting shoes can cause a horse to falter in stride, stumble badly, fall, or otherwise lose precious seconds while he compensates for the uncomfortable or unbalanced sensation; and any of these can result in (at best) a limited performance or (at worst) a serious racing accident that may involve other horses and riders.

The legs of a racer are always suspected problem areas, due to the extreme stress put on them during an extended effort, and so are subject to constant surveillance, particularly before a hard run.

Too, there are such automatic duties as checking the horse's eyes for bruises or foreign objects. A horse that catches a flying clod of dirt in his eye in the morning may have trouble by afternoon if it isn't attended to quickly. There is always the chance that he may be struck by a lump of earth during the afternoon race, too, but by then there is nothing to be done about it.

Beau always concentrated his personal attention on the tack, although his saddle was kept in the Jock's Room and carefully tended by his valet. This man was also responsible for Beau's racing silks or colors, his breeches, helmet, boots, and whips, while the exercise boys were in charge of caring for the daily tack. But, as Beau's life might some day depend on a worn piece of leather or a faulty buckle, he always made it his business to check everything thoroughly. As both contract rider and exercise boy for Deepwater, he had access to the bridles his mounts would wear as well as all their other equipment, and was able to inspect his gear without overtly insulting anyone else's care and judgment.

In sharp contrast to Monty's pensive mood, both Beau and Drop Cord moved easily about their work, humming bits of popular tunes or whistling medleys of calypso songs. Their apparent nonchalance and lack of worry about the upcoming stake was more than Monty could endure. Finally, as all three were passing through the tack room, he pointed at the *Racing News* and asked sarcastically, "Has either of you happy hooligans taken a look at the paper this morning?"

"Sure" was the two-person, one-grunt answer.

"And did you happen to notice what the field looks like for the Marquesa, that you're so blasted free of care?" Without pausing for an answer, he went on, his voice rising. "If you did, then you realize that we're up against six of the toughest mares this side of Gallorette and Shuvee! And that four of 'em have the kind of early speed that makes you *have* to run with them, and two of those four are capable of burning up the racetrack from wire to wire! And as if there wasn't trouble enough with them on the front end, you have one dyed-in-the-wool, genuine, come-from-behind horse, with a closing run in her that would make a cheetah look sick!"

"But—"

"Add one more freight train who doesn't care how she runs and is just as happy to run with colts, and your sum total is trouble with a capital *T!*"

"Whoa up a minute and hold 'er right there!" Beau spoke with authority and even Monty backed off a step. "Ain't you forgetting a few things about what *we* have to offer? Like a top-drawer runner who beat everything there was to beat when she was running? Like a mare with a heart as big as a drum and the class to go with it? Not a horse in that field gonna stay with her when she goes to running, you wait and see! She's fresh and she's ready, and when she makes her move I guarantee she'll run by them like they was stopped!"

Drop Cord grinned clear up to the tops of his eyebrows. "You know, boss, she's fit as a horse could be to go this distance. Her legs are ice cold, without whirlpooling or anything else, and solid as four tree trunks. She works and she comes back tight, barely turns a hair and hardly blows. She's ready, boss. As ready as any horse will ever be. Haven't *I* been takin' care of her for you? No sir, don't you shred up your nerves about Bonnie. She'll pass those mares like they was turned to marble. She'll just go to the front and improve her position!"

"You two are so sure of yourselves, it's disgusting,"

said Monty. "I wish I could be that positive. If I didn't think she had a pretty fair chance, I wouldn't let her run, but you know as well as I do, how it is with older horses. So much can happen during a race, and if anything happens to her . . . well, it can't! Julie believes that Bonnie can beat anything they run at her, and you two are all revved up on the same fool notion; I'm trying to be realistic and not underestimate the competition. Overconfidence has lost many a good horse a race that he should have had in his feedbag." Monty spread the past-performance charts out on the tack trunks and motioned the two men over. "Let's look at these together."

The three men pored over the charts for the better part of an hour, discussing the probable running strategy of each of the entrants as indicated by their previous races. Each chart showed the last ten races that the horse had run, and included the date, distance, and conditions under which every race was run (such as allowance, handicap, name of a stakes race, or the amount of a claiming tag); the post position, weight carried, jockey's name, order of the first three finishers, and a comment on the horse's performance—cryptic, informative phrases like "ridden out," "gamely," "driving," "early speed," "tired," "rallied," "gave way," "no mishap," "bad start," and a host of others.

The chart also gave the number of starts the horse had made during the past two years, how often he had finished first, second, or third, and his total annual earnings. Each horse was identified by name, color, sex, age, sire, dam, and sire of dam; as well as by breeder, current owner, trainer, and state in which he was foaled.

However, the most interesting parts of any chart are those that show the horse's position at the points of call during a race—the quarter pole, the half-mile mark, the stretch, and others, depending on the distance of the race; and the fractions for the horse in the lead at the quarter pole, half-mile pole, and finish. By noting, for example, that a particular race at six furlongs was run in one minute ten and two-fifths seconds, with fractions of :22–3/5, :45, 1:10–2/5, and that the horse in question is shown as being 1, 2^{hd}, 2^{hd}, 1^{hd}, 1–3/4, a trainer can learn a great deal about the horse's running style. He will understand that the horse broke on top, was second by a head at the quarter pole behind the leader (who got there in 22–3/5 seconds), and so on. By studying this data for ten races, an astute trainer can see the horse's running pattern quite clearly, and thus evaluate his own animal's opposition with a high degree of accuracy.

"Okay," said Monty at last, excitement in his tone for the first time, "then we're all agreed. We can discount Laughable's last race as a fluke, and look for her to break on top as usual with the help of the number one post. Merrie Millie won't be as fast out of the number two slot and will drop back off the pace at least as far as the half. We're in number three, and can probably drop in on the rail before the clubhouse turn, provided that Bookmark doesn't make a bid for the same spot. But Beau, you ride it as you see it. To do that, Bookmark will have to cross in front of you, which is possible 'cause she's greased lightning coming out of the box. Sweet Sundae will wait for things to sort themselves out in front of her, and likely won't be driving for a hole to the rail; but you'll have to watch out for her later on. Little Nell is in the six, and that one is just eligible to run away from everybody, but the outside post won't help her and she'll be looking to save ground toward the inside just as soon as she can. That leaves Ruby Frump in the seven, and she's the real sleeper. If she runs back to her form in the Pilgrim Handicap, everyone will have a run for his money. If she stops, as she has the last two times out, nobody'll know she's around. Whichever way it goes, we're in a pretty good spot, and as long as those firecrackers don't get too much of an edge at the start, I think you'll find you have all the horse you need."

Beau and Drop Cord nodded their assent, exchanging a wink over Monty's head. "*We* were agreed before you started," said Beau. "Now that you've joined us, the vote's unanimous." He looked at his watch. "Got an errand to run before I report to the Jock's Room. See you in the winner's circle!"

The Marquesa was the feature race of the day, and was therefore scheduled seventh on the card. Post time for the seventh was always four o'clock. At three fifteen, Julie arrived on the race track grounds in an ambulance, and soon was braced securely in a wheelchair which was carefully pushed by Dirk Markham, with Rand Jefferson walking alongside with his eye on his daughter.

This would be the first time that Julie would not be in the paddock while Bonnie was being saddled, but with the wheelchair it would have been much too dangerous for both the girl and the horses. Instead, Rand had arranged with the Kandahar officials, many of whom were old friends of Julie's, for her and the entire Deepwater contingent to view the race from the infield, in order to have the most unobstructed view with the least maneuvering.

They arrived in time to see the horses warming up for the sixth race. There was a slight delay as the nine horse balked at the starting gate, but after some prodding and the firm hand of an assistant starter on his bridle, he entered the box. In the blink of an eye, the starter scanned his line-up; with clanging bell and mechanical snap, the doors flew open and the horses charged forward.

It does not take long to run six furlongs, even with bad horses. In less than a minute and eleven seconds, the race was over, the horses came jogging back to be unsaddled. The winner posed momentarily for his photograph. The results were declared official.

As the steaming horses were led from the track, Julie narrowed her sun-dazzled eyes in the direction of the stable area, watching for the first arrivals for the seventh race.

Knowing that Julie would be anxious, Drop Cord had timed his trip to the paddock down to the last second. He listened carefully to the announcer calling the sixth race, and managed to approach the gap and the man handing out the numbers just as the latter lifted the barrier to permit entrance onto the track. Had he been a few seconds earlier, Bonnie would have had to wait while the horses in the sixth race rounded the turn and made the final run for the wire; in all likelihood, the big mare would have become agitated and upset at the delay. Now, though, thanks to the groom's flawless timing, the man simply snapped her number onto her bit (indicating that she was the horse in the number three post position), and Drop Cord proceeded down the track to the saddling paddock without a break in his stride. He located Julie and her escorts in the infield, and waved his hat in greeting.

"Oh, doesn't she look wonderful?" Julie smiled up at her father and Dirk, the loving pride she had in her mare eclipsing everything else for the moment.

"Never better," they agreed heartily, both wishing that the same could be said for the girl.

Ten minutes later, the announcer's voice boomed over the p-a system. "The horses are coming onto the track. Ladies and gentlemen, you have twelve minutes to place your bets on the seventh race. Post time will be four-oh-six."

As the horses paraded forth, even Julie had to admit to herself that they were an impressive group and not simply an unimportant escort for her own mare. Every one was a multiple stakes winner. All but Sunbonnet had been running more or less constantly for several years. Not a one had ever been laid off for any serious ailment—again, excepting Bonnie—and the oldest of her competition was aged five.

They turned in front of the grandstand, following the outrider as he led them back up the track. Now some of the horses began to jog and gallop, long easy strides that loosened taut muscles and started all the marvelous gears to meshing. Beau held Bonnie to a steady, prancing walk beside Moriarty's stolid replacement until they were almost in front of Julie. Then he flicked his whip to his cap and spoke just loudly enough for the girl to hear. "Exactly two minutes, one and three-fifths seconds after those doors open, I'll meet you in the winner's circle. Don't be late!" With that, he stood in his irons and let Bonnie move off at her rhythmic, ground-gulping canter, while Moriarty's pinto stand-in tried valiantly to stay by her side.

The last of the horses drifted on around the turn, and at a signal from one of the patrol judges, a small group crossed the track into the infield. Rollin Tolkov, the plump and jovial owner of Deepwater and Fieldstone Farms as well as a giant industrial complex and more money than Julie had ever been able to imagine, led the little column, followed closely by Monty and Drop Cord.

"My dear girl," said Mr. T, grasping both her hands and staring into her pale face, "oh, my dear child, how are you?" He had arrived from New York only half an hour before.

"I'm a *lot* better now," said Julie, clenching his fingers tightly. She owed more to this man than she felt she could ever repay, although Mr. T himself considered that he was her debtor. "It's grand to have you home!"

Drop Cord, hanging back for a minute or two after

his initial greeting, studied the big mare intently as she stretched her legs and flexed her muscles. Then, quietly, almost shyly, he stepped forward and spoke for Julie's ears alone. "Ain't nothing out there can catch her today. She'll run a hole in the wind, she will."

Julie smiled. "A hole in the wind. I like that, Drop Cord. It sounds like the way she runs."

"The horses are nearing the starting gate," the announcer said in his amplified, impersonal fashion, and an increasing tide of people pressed closer to the fence.

Monty gave her shoulder a light squeeze. "They won't beat that three horse, lady, and that's the truth. I got it straight from the horse's mouth."

The first four horses were standing quietly in the gate. Julie glanced back at Monty, a little wide-eyed. "That's the first time you ever predicted success without an *if* or *unless*," she told him.

Number five went in without protest, while six began to give her rider trouble. An assistant starter grabbed her bridle before she could become a real problem and guided her into the starting stall. Seven loaded like the trouper she was, and then for a moment looked as if she would try to back right out.

"Mike, get in there with the seven." The starter spoke softly into his microphone. A wiry red-haired man in the khaki uniform of an assistant starter wedged himself into the seventh stall and pulled the mare's head straight.

"Not ready."

"Wait a minute."

"No chance here." The jockeys' voices floated past the little group in the infield.

"In all your years, Drop Cord, have you ever heard a jock say, 'I'm ready'?" Monty asked.

"Nope. Never."

"It just isn't done," said Rand.

"Straighten up the one," the starter said. The boy on the one horse gave a swift tug on a rein, bringing the mare's head into perfect position. Almost instantly the starter released the button of the extension cord he held, and amidst great whooping and yelling from the jockeys, which all but drowned out the ringing bells, the gates sprang open and the race was on.

As expected, Laughable and Little Nell were first out of the gate, leading the rest of the field by nearly a length in less than an eighth of a mile. Merrie Millie made a surprising bid for the number two spot on the rail, leaving Sunbonnet and Ruby Frump matching strides as they vied for position. Bookmark broke poorly, taking several awkward jumps before settling into stride, while Sweet Sundae made her way to the rail, trailing the field.

Approaching the clubhouse turn, Beau tightened his hold on Bonnie, barely avoiding a traffic jam as Merrie Millie drifted out from the rail and Ruby Frump closed in to save ground. Seeing the hole left open by the wide-running Millie, Sweet Sundae made a mild bid for the spot, forcing Bonnie to check slightly in close quarters to avoid either clipping the heels of the second-place Millie or bumping the close-running Ruby Frump to her right.

They continued that way around the turn, with Laughable and Little Nell dueling for the lead, while Merrie Millie moved up to challenge. Sundae and Frump were running easily, neither willing to give ground in any direction, and in so doing managed to keep Bonnie in a blind switch between them and behind the pace-forcing Millie.

"Well now lookie here, girl friend! Broadway and Forty-Second Street for sure!" Beau whispered to the horse running effortlessly beneath him. "We'll just hang

in here for a little longer and see if somethin' doesn't
open up for us."

The rhythmic stride continued flawlessly for another
furlong, as Little Nell began to tire from the pressure of
the blistering pace, allowing Laughable to gain a three-
quarter-length lead. At the half-mile mark, it was all
that Beau could do to restrain the big mare, and with
the flagging Little Nell added to the challenging Millie,
Sundae, and Ruby Frump, the bunch of horses formed a
wall in front of him, offering no racing room in which to
make a move.

"Hang on, Gumdrop, a little touch longer, there's my
bonbon. They'll give us a hole to squeeze through."

But the big mare was not to be held in. She knew
what she wanted to do, and 123 pounds of Beau Watkins were not about to deter her. With determination,
she began to lengthen her stride, reaching far beyond
her for vast chunks of ground and gulping them whole
without pausing. Before her, Sweet Sundae let a crack of
light show through as Ruby Frump edged her by a head,
and in a flash the fluid bay had threaded herself through
the narrow space to gain a head on both.

Little Nell was failing rapidly, causing the horses behind her either to take back or to go around her heaving
flanks, while Merrie Millie gained command from the
fast-tiring Laughable. Despite Bonnie's move beween
horses that put her a neck to the good, Ruby Frump was
far from finished and rallied strongly in the middle of the
track to battle head and head with Millie for the lead.

Suddenly, Bonnie had had enough of this foolishness.
Checkers might be all right for rainy afternoons in the
tack room, jump here, jump there, move little
distances . . . but this was horse racing, and her business was to run. Still under restraint from Beau, who
had no intention of making a move before the quarter pole, she forged ahead with speed to spare, sweep-

ing past the laboring Laughable and the battling leaders as if they had suddenly frozen in their tracks.

As they rounded the turn into the stretch, she had established a four-length lead and was steadily drawing away. Bookmark, who had trailed the field for the first half, made a strong late bid, running wide around tiring horses to hook up with Ruby Frump in the stretch; for a moment it seemed that she might make a run at the flying bay haunches, but there was really no chance. Sunbonnet, still running under wraps, was straining to be free of the steady hands that begged her to ease off. With less than a sixteenth of a mile to go, she had increased her lead to fifteen lengths.

The crowd was irrepressibly wild as she crossed the wire alone, more than seventeen lengths in front of Bookmark, who finished a nose before the game Ruby Frump.

The tote board registered the time of the race. Two minutes, one and three-fifths seconds.

"Dad, look! Look, everybody!" screamed Julie Jefferson. *"She's knocked two-fifths of a second off the track record!"*

Rand carefully wheeled a tearfully joyous girl to the winner's circle, flanked by Mr. T. and Dirk Monty and Drop Cord had already run out onto the track to meet Bonnie and Beau. As the entire group posed in the circle for the traditional *win* photo, a large silver plate was set gently on Julie's lap by a smiling, gray-haired woman whose grandfather had owned and bred the great mare Marquesa for whom the stakes race was named. Julie was too overcome by the emotion of that moment to utter a single word.

When at last she did speak, it was to her beloved mare, as she patted the out-stretched muzzle and smiled mistily. "Bonnie, dear Bonnie. It was just like they said: 2:01-3/5 and there was no one to catch you. They said you would and you did. You ran a hole in the wind!"

Chapter EIGHT

On Sunday morning, every member of Mr. T's far-flung crew was in high spirits: from Kandahar Park to Fieldstone Farm, from Deepwater to Chambers Memorial Hospital, jubilation was rampant. Not only had Bonnie won as decisive a victory as possible in the Marquesa, but she had come out of the race in perfect condition, her legs cold and no signs of stress anywhere.

"The papers said she 'won as she pleased,' " Beau reported, "and they're right! I was only along for the ride."

"Told you so," said Stash to Leon.

"*You* did! Why, *I* told *you!*" said Leon to Stash.

"Greatest horse ever foaled," said Scorchy to Peaches. "Knew it from the minute I saw her work that first morning."

"There was never any doubt in my mind," said Pop to his friend Tweedy, who had sired Bonnie's twins, "that she'd take the Marquesa. Sure as the crows fly back to China every year. Or whoever flies where. No doubt whatever."

And Dan Gibson was on the phone to his uncle, passing along the news of the race furlong by furlong, and stuttering with renewed excitement on the turns.

Monty, meanwhile, on the basis of her startling performance, had already scrutinized the book of stakes races for the Kandahar Spring Meeting and selected another trial for her—the Dresden Handicap—besides lining up several others, each one contingent on the previous race. Once again the distance would be a mile and a quarter, open to mares four years old and up. The purse was $75,000 added, and the ease with which she had put away six of the best mares in the country made Monty feel that the $5,000 supplemental nomination fee was a worthwhile investment.

He announced his intentions to Julie at the hospital, amid a detailed review of Bonnie's post-race condition that covered nearly every hair from nose to tail. Rand read glowing accounts of the mare's spectacular win from at least four sports sections, besides the two full columns afforded the race in the Sunday edition of the *Racing News,* and proudly exhibited to nurses, doctors, aides, and visitors its photo of Bonnie alone at the wire.

Naturally Julie was delighted, her enthusiasm for everything concerning the big bay flushing her cheeks with color and sparkling in her eyes. Her physician came in and found her looking, as he said at once, healthier than any of the staff. He had been discussing her case with the therapist, and the surprising improvement in everything except her ability to walk that had been wrought, obviously, by the exalted state of mind into which the race had put her.

"I was going to keep you here for four or five days longer," he said, "but I see no reason to do that now. I've had a long talk with your father, who's something of a medical man himself—"

"Mainly with animals, mind," said Rand hastily.

"Well, at any rate, he knows what to do for you, so

I'm not even going to give you the full-time nurse for
two weeks that I'd intended. Once a week the therapist
will visit you to check on your progress and work out
your exercise schedule. I'll expect to see you here a few
times for check-ups; I'll let you know when. I believe
you'll improve without that operation I mentioned. If
you don't . . . well, you mustn't cross bridges till
you've reached them. I'll be sending crutches home with
you, and you'll learn the use of 'em there. The metal
ones, you know, with the armbands?"

"Yes, I've seen them. How long do you think it'll be
till that pressure is wholly released?" the girl asked him
hesitantly.

"A pure guess: two or three months. Don't count on
it or hold me to it. It's a hopeful guess."

"Why can't I have the old-fashioned Long John Silver
wooden crutches?"

"On those, the swing-your-legs-through kind, your
weight's all on your hands. No good. On the chrome
steel crutches, you can gait-walk rather than swing your
body. Not so picturesque, but practical."

"And when can I leave?"

"Any time after eight A.M. tomorrow."

"Wonderful! Is two minutes after eight all right?"
He nodded, grinned, and left them.

"Great," said Monty. "Now your car's in Ohio, Rand,
so I'll have Dan drive me to Deepwater, and I'll pick up
Julie's car and drive it back. Collect you two here tomorrow morning—"

"At two minutes after eight," said Julie.

"And you'll drop me off at Kandahar. Take off for
Deepwater, collect the dogs, however many of them
there are by now, and go home to the cottage at Fieldstone."

"Why not Deepwater?" asked Rand Jefferson. "Her

apartment there is bigger than the whole cottage at Fieldstone."

"Yes, but it's up a flight of stairs. Julie'd better be confined to ground level till she gets her climbing legs back in shape."

"Besides," said the girl, "Tam and Deer, Bonnie's twins, are living at Fieldstone. And Croydon's close by, where Cache is staying with Dirk."

Monty attempted with small success to look happy about that; he'd forgotten Dirk for the moment.

With the homegoing plans arranged, the young trainer headed back to Kandahar to check on the horses, call Dan Gibson to ask him for the loan of a couple of hours of driving time, and finally to tell the good news to Drop Cord and anyone else who might happen to be in Barn 7 at four thirty on a Sunday afternoon.

"Just like they say," Drop Cord told him philosophically, "the bad 'n' the good always comes in threes."

"How's that?"

"Well, first Julie got hurt, then Moriarty was a casualty, then Julie was gettin' better and found out she couldn't walk. That's three calamities in any fellow's book."

"I guess you could see it that way," said Monty, and lifted an eyebrow at the groom's intent expression, which obviously mirrored a total belief in what he'd said.

"Then Bonnie won the Marquesa—'all by herself'— 'goin' away' if you please—then she come outa that race better than ever, and right behind that, Julie's allowed to go home!" The big man smiled at his own logical reasoning. "If that ain't three good happenings, I'm third cousin to a Percheron!"

"No, I'd guess a Clydesdale. . . . Does that mean we're now in for three more disasters?" asked Monty, sounding serious so that he wouldn't offend the big man's earnest philosophy.

"Not at all. Just shows you it all runs in threes. Why, you ask anybody in show business—they know it better'n anybody. Everything comes in threes. You can keep runnin' in good sets forever, or in bad, but it'll always play out at the end of a three."

"Then let's hope that the first in our next triple play will be a favorable assignment of weight for the Dresden Handicap. I'm afraid the Racing Secretary will take one look at the Marquesa and weight us right out of contention. After all, that's what happened to Man o' War: they retired him because he had to carry more weight than any racehorse had ever been assigned before. And I do, after the Marquesa I really *do* begin to believe that Sunbonnet is the greatest horse alive." He sighed. "Oh, I expect top weight, of course, but I only hope that it isn't absurd!"

"Sec'tary could always make you give the others a fifteen-length head start," said Drop Cord with an almost straight face. "I don't figure that'd make a lot of difference to her. She'd just get down to the business of runnin' a little earlier. She'd beat 'em just the same."

"Sure thing," said Monty, knowing how useless it was to argue with Drop Cord, Beau, or Julie on the subject of Bonnie's unknown limitations. "They make quite a threesome themselves," he said to himself, "talking of things coming in threes."

Monty began his Monday as usual at the track, and after checking Bonnie thoroughly, both in and out of the stall, and watching several sets gallop, he left everything else in the capable hands of his men and drove off to the hospital.

Julie had had a lengthy session with her doctor, which included a list of instructions that she swore to follow to

the letter. At the appointed hour she was wheeled to the
desk, where Rand signed her out, and came forth into
warm May sunshine at precisely eight two.

"Oh, isn't it a gorgeous day! Can't you fairly smell
horses on the breeze? And fresh grass and puppies'
clean coats?"

"In the middle of town?" said Monty.

"Sure," said Rand, "why not?"

Monty sniffed hard. "Great heavens," he said mildly,
"I think you're right."

"Could I visit Bonnie for just a few minutes when we
drop you off?" asked Julie eagerly.

"Nope," said Rand.

"Better not," said Monty.

"But——"

"No buts, for once in your life," said Monty. "You
have a long drive to Fieldstone. You have a pit stop on
the way, to accumulate your dogs at Deepwater, too.
That's more than enough for you in one day. How many
dogs are you taking, anyway?"

"All of them, naturally. Pushy, Nana, Barney, and
the black pup."

"I'm grateful you're leaving Bonnie in my dubious
care," said Monty.

"Wouldn't if I didn't have to," she said airily. "Drive
on, Montgomery."

They let him out at the stable gate, where he promised to call Julie nightly to report on Bonnie's progress
as well as the affairs of the day, and to deliver his news
in person every Saturday. Rand, shaking his hand as he
took over the wheel, silently wondered whether the
nearness of Dirk Markham might perhaps force the shy
trainer into some sort of action. Yes, he'd be watching
developments on that front with interest. Rand had
known and liked Monty since the latter's boyhood, but
Markham was quite a man too. And it was past time for

Julie to begin thinking of something besides horses and dogs. . . .

Monty walked back to Barn 7, whistling. Life was looking up at last. Julie was on her way home, the doctor optimistic on the results of therapy. Bonnie was perfect. And Monty Everett had just made up his mind to ask Julie Jefferson to marry him.

Saturday would be the day. He'd spend the week rehearsing his speech ("Is this 1875, or a hundred years later?" he asked himself derisively; yet he knew very well that he *would* concoct a speech, and that somehow he *would* manage to deliver it to Julie).

All the horses had been out when he reached the shed, and only two of the gallopers were still cooling out. Bonnie had been walked for forty minutes around the shed, and had then been allowed to graze for another twenty before returning to her stall. She would walk one more day—three days in all—before resuming her routine of galloping. Monty smiled with satisfaction. "It's about time we had a run of decent luck," he told himself, going in to mark the charts for Tuesday's work with Dan Gibson.

"Attention horsemen! Attention horsemen!" the p-a system interrupted the morning sounds of the backstretch. "Trainer Justin Wells, telephone message at he Secretary's office. Trainers Foster Garnett and Dominic Rocco, please report to the Racing Secretary's office. Trainer Montgomery Everett, please report to the stewards' office. Attention horsemen! Attention—"

"Wonder what they want?" said Monty.

"Probably want you to fill a race for them," said Dan. "Lord knows, you run more than your fair share, and still when they come up short you're the first to be asked."

"The stewards don't fill races," said Monty, puzzled.

"I'd best hightail it over there to see what's on their minds."

He covered the short distance to the administrative building in a few minutes and went directly to the offices of the Racing Commission. A young secretary took his name, announced his arrival to a small intercom, and ushered him through a dark and heavy oaken door into the office of Larry O'Neill, one of three men who comprised the Board of Stewards for the Kandahar meeting. (A Board of Stewards is usually made up of three members: one appointed by the State Racing Commission, one by the racetrack—in this instance, the Kandahar Racing Association—and a third selected with the approval of both.)

"Morning, Larry! What can I do for you?"

Larry O'Neill had known Monty for the better part of twenty years. An ex-jockey who'd decided to go into the administrative branch of racing after a serious fall, in his days as a top race rider he had ridden for Will Everett, Monty's father; and later he'd become a close friend of their family, well before the senior Everett retired to St. Clair Farm and Monty decided to make training his career. He was a short, ugly, wire-and-leather man who'd kept his fighting weight and his crisp jock's manner into his middle years. He looked up at Monty with a grin, half welcoming, half embarrassed, on his monkey face.

"Hallo, youngster. Sit. You look chipper." He fidgeted with papers, uncharacteristically. "I don't know where to begin," he said plaintively.

"What is it?"

"Monty, ah, look, is there anything you'd like to say about Sunbonnet's uh-ah-err *fantastic* finish on Saturday?"

"Just that it was fantastic," said Monty blankly. "What are you getting at?" Monty's happy mood had been swiped away and a cold small hand clutched his stomach while another began tying knots in his throat. "What could I possibly tell you that you don't already know from seeing the race and the films? She broke well, saved ground, got in a box—"

"No, that isn't what I mean. Feel like a blurry fool. Lemme put it this way. Ah. Yes, come right out with it." The ex-rider sat up straight and scowled. "If you're using any drugs on that mare that might be illegal in this state, stop it right away. And for good."

Monty was on his feet again, though he didn't know it. "What are you handing me, Larry?" All his blood seemed to be in his head, rage mixed with bewilderment spinning his brain around behind the scarlet face. "I've never used, I *would* never use, I have no reason to use any drugs on Bonnet!"

"Easy does it, son. This is only a warning."

"Because she set a new track record and left all the others sitting on their horseshoes, you're warning me not to use drugs on her? You're saying that I did? Larry, I—"

"We got the results today from the lab on the spit-box and urine samples from Saturday's races. Sunbonnet came up with a cloudy test on the urine."

"WHAT!" roared Monty.

"No specific drug's been identified, so this is as far as it goes. This time. But you'd better make sure that you're not giving her anything that might test positive in the box. That's all I'm telling you, son. No accusations. Just check the ingredients in her vitamins or tonics or feed supplements. Make sure you stop all medication at least seventy-two hours before you run her."

"Larry, how long have you known me? Do you honestly believe that I'm—that Will Everett's boy isn't aware of all the rules covering drugs and medications in every state I race in? Do you think I'd be so stupid, dumb, foolish, pumpkinheaded, as to take a chance with a horse like this one? Or *any* horse? Larry, believe me:

this mare doesn't get anything except hay, oats, Tri-Crown sweet feed, a little bran, and 910 supplement. Same as every other horse in the shed. Nothing more. Nothing less. Nothing to cloud any kind of test!"

Monty stopped shouting. It came over him in a sick wave: there had been other trainers whose horses had come back with cloudy or positive tests, who protested their innocence loudly. He, like most other witnesses, had looked on such vehement protestations as necessary, but had always secretly wondered whether those trainers hadn't been "giving their horses a little help" and been caught in the process. It had seldom occurred to him that indeed their horses might not have been given anything, at least by the trainers or their stable help. And it always seemed a pretty lame excuse to say that someone unknown from outside the stable might have doped a trainer's horse, too. Now he began to speculate on how many of those fellows had been wrongly accused.

"Larry," he tried again, "I don't know why that test came back cloudy. But I swear to you that I never have and never will give a horse anything that could possibly be on the list of forbidden substances. You have to believe that."

"Wait a minute, Monty. I said I'm not blaming you for any illegal act. In fact, unless they sent back a test marked 'positive' for a specific, named drug, *no one* can charge you with anything."

"But—"

"And I'm not saying that you personally administered anything to Sunbonnet. But a trainer's wholly responsible for the horses he runs. You know that as well as I do. And something made that test come back cloudy! Inconclusive, but definitely not clean. So it's my duty to tell you about it."

"At least I'm glad it's you, Larry, and not a stranger.

You must have a good idea that I'm telling you the truth."

"Of course I do. I want to give you a chance to check up on a few items. What about your help? Your grooms, exercise boys, hot-walkers? Are they reliable? How long have you known them? Is there any one of them who'd have reason to try to insure a win in that race? Did anybody at all have doubts of the mare's ability to come out in front? What about the jockey? He's a contract man, isn't he? And—"

"This is insane," said Monty between his teeth. "I've had the same crew for more than two years. You'll admit that's rather a record at the track. The newest employee is my head groom, and he's been with me for two years and five months. As for the jock, that's an even wilder idea. Don't you know Beau?" Larry shook his head. "He's Stash Watkins' boy. Stash worked for Dad for—for more than a quarter of a century, I think it must be; and Beau was raised with me. As a matter of fact, the only soul who was worried over Bonnie's chances was me! The others were always sure . . ." He left the words hanging in the air, hearing them again as though someone else had said them.

"Yes? The others were over-confident, then, about the mare's chances?" asked the steward tonelessly.

"Not over-confident. They just always seem to think that that mare can do anything. But then, so does her owner, who was still this morning flat on her back in a hospital bed, which I think eliminates her from your list of suspects."

"Monty, no need to steam your ears over this. I'm doing my job."

The trainer subsided into a chair. "Sorry, Larry. I know it. I just don't understand. Cloudy test . . . I don't get it."

"Since there's no positive identification of drugs or

medications," O'Neill went on, "the purse distribution will remain as is; the first-place money will be credited to your account this morning. If your shed gang's as trustworthy as you claim, son, I'd seriously consider putting your mare under lock and key, or hiring a special guard, or sleeping in her stall yourself, the next time you get ready to run her. Because if what you say is true, then the only answer is outside interference, and if they got away with it once, they might try again."

"*If* what I say is true?"

"Some of it isn't proof, Monty. It's your opinion. Never been wrong before?" Larry asked mildly.

"Not about my own men, no."

"You're the only perfect judge of men I ever met, then. Your father must be proud of you."

Monty lowered at him for a minute. Then he capitulated. "Okay, nobody can vouch for anyone but himself one hundred percent. But I'm doing it. If one of my boys did anything wrong, I'll take the entire responsibility."

"You have to," Larry reminded him, "whether you want to or not."

"Right. I didn't mean to go all righteous on you, but this is a really *good* bunch I have. I don't know where to begin to look for the reason for this, Larry, but I'll do something. And you have my thanks."

"Good. When will you run that mare again?"

"I'm about to enter her in the Dresden, twelve days from today. Mark that date on your calendar, old friend, and go and watch the bay bombshell run away from the field as if she'd stolen something. That'll give the lab another shot at her."

"Best of luck," said the steward as the door closed behind Monty. It had a curiously hollow ring.

Outside, Monty paced off toward the shed row, trying to settle his whirling, tumbling thoughts into an orderly arrangement. Taking each idea separately, he established three categories: Impossible, Highly Improbable, and Ridiculous. By the time he'd reached the shed he had calmed himself into coherence, and immediately called a council in the tack room. In a few moments all his own reactions were being duplicated by his crew: shock, disbelief, outrage, puzzlement, righteous indignation, and back to shock again. The room buzzed with protests, with statements of general and individual innocence, with vague but fierce criticisms of inefficient testing procedures, probable mix-ups, and so forth; with incredulity that Deepwater Farm could be even suspected of such a crime, and with astonishment that they could ever have been caught up in such an indefensible situation.

"Now we're not totally without recourse in a case of definite positive results," Monty told them. "A trainer has the right to a hearing before the State Racing Commission, and may also institute court proceedings if he's certain of his innocence and believes he can prove it."

"You mean if it happens again?" asked someone, appalled.

"Yes. This time it's all right."

"Well, you'd have to be almighty fast on the trigger to stop 'em from redistributin' the purse," said Drop Cord solemnly. "Though, now I think on it, they did get stopped with the Kentucky Derby winner, few years back; the money was put into an account that paid int'rest by the racetrack, till the case'ld be decided. Dragged through the courts for near four years." He shook his head.

"What happened?" asked Marsh.

"They held up the original decision. Took the winner's number down, credited the second horse with the win. *And* the purse."

"Well, you can bet your next ten stakes that I'd fight

them to the finish," said Monty. "Bonnie and every other horse under this shed runs on her own. If one needs drugs to run, then either we cure whatever ails it before it sets hoof on the track, or we send it home. Deepwater Farm," he went on, getting mad all over again, "doesn't need to get speed and stamina and courage out of a bottle, jar, or can; and the day that we do is the day I'll hang it all up and start raising flowers for a living. Or knitting argyle socks."

"Me too," said Beau.

"No sir, this is one time I'm sure. We sent Bonnie into the Marquesa straight and clean. Nobody had anything to gain by trying to move her up for the win, and if it was the other way around and they'd tried to stop her, she'd never have won as impressively as she did, right? Besides, she didn't *need* anything extra. You both told me that yourselves." He looked at the jockey and the groom. "It's only that both of you neglected to prophesy this minor disaster."

Becoming more incensed by the moment as he thought over the whole matter, Monty's fist slammed down on a tack trunk and his voice rose as his temper flared. "Nobody even cared whether the mare won, not to any extent! There's never been any pressure about her at all! Certainly Mr. T couldn't care less, so long as she pulled up okay—that's how he is with all the string. And I hardly see the cashing of a big bet as any motivation, do you? With the public betting her down to two-to-one in spite of her long vacation from the track. No! In fact, the only person who really cared about her winning the Marquesa was Julie!"

There was a longish silence.

"And me, on account of Julie," said Beau quietly.

"And me, same reason," said Drop Cord.

"And me," said almost everyone loyally.

"And me," said Monty very slowly, "on Julie's account. Yes. Well. Hmm." He caught himself talking like Larry O'Neill and coughed. "I know, anyway, that none of us would have given Bonnie an artificial edge. We all knew she didn't need it, right?"

"What you gonna tell Julie about this?" murmured Drop Cord, whose huge face was as glum as a graveyard on a wet Thursday.

"I haven't decided. I think I won't mention it. There's nothing we can *do* about it, after all. No use in her worrying."

"I go along with that," said Beau.

However, along with the best-laid plans of dice and wrens, as Stash was wont to say, this small act of kindness was not to be allowed to succeed. The following morning, the late city edition of the *Daily Herald* hit the stands with a several-column article that included a brief rundown of Bonnie's seventeen-length runaway in the Marquesa, the report of Monty's summons to the steward's office, and some pretty strong speculation on the return of inconclusive lab reports as well as the many possibilities and properties of specific drugs that might account for such an outstanding performance in a horse. There were implications—no quite libelous, but not quite *un*libelous—that challenged Monty's integrity and the success he'd had with the Deepwater horses. There were even backhand swipes at Deepwater's impeccable reputation and at Rollin Tolkov himself.

The writer responsible was a relative newcomer to the reporting of racing news, and obviously thought that he had uncovered a dramatic scoop. His performance was set down in front of Monty by Dan Gibson, who was fully as livid as Monty was about to become.

"That dirty atrocity-committing lunatic! That backstabbing lying idiot! What kind of fool would write this mess on such thin provocation, and what kind of a rag would print it?" His howls of wrath brought his gang on the run. The paper was snatched from hand to hand till it lay in tatters on the floor, while everyone talked or shouted at once.

"Better get to Fieldstone fast, boss," said Beau thickly. "You don't want Julie and her dad to hear this from somebody else—or maybe see the *Herald* themselves."

"Man, you are right." Monty hauled himself together and assigned duties at the top of his lungs, shot for his car, and was on his way.

A few minutes later a telephone call came in for him from New York, which Dan Gibson took: it was Mr. T himself. "What about this, Dan?" he asked levelly. Dan told him all that he knew. "Well," said Mr. T at last, "pass this word along, Dan. I don't believe for a minute that Sunbonnet was doped. But if she was, I don't believe for five seconds that any of your crew had a hand in it; I don't know them all personally, I admit, but Monty Everett does, and I have absolute faith in his judgment and integrity. You can tell him for me that the instant I hang up this phone, I'll have my lawyers on the neck of this so-called 'news' paper, and they'll see what can be done about apologies, retractions, and all that. Meantime," Mr. T took a large breath, "all of you try not to fret about it. I'm sure it will all clear itself up."

The phone went dead. Dan hung up slowly. "I sure hope you're right, sir," he said under his breath. "I don't like the feel of it. Not one little bit, I don't. I have a hunch the clouds have only begun to gather."

He went alone to stare at Bonnie in her stall. "Gumdrop," he said, "somebody's gone and betrayed you. They didn't trust you to win on your own. I wish I knew who it was." He looked down at his hands. He was a mild, decent man; but now he said hoarsely, "I think I'd kill 'em!"

Chapter *NINE*

On his way to Fieldstone Monty had determined to tell Rand and Julie the whole story in chronological order. There were too many loose ends and possibilities and dilemmas for a man to just start off with the main problem. Yes, he was going to start with Larry O'Neill. . . .

As always, his thoughtful plan had been made without taking into account one of the greatest obstacles to the full uninterrupted telling of a story: Julie Jefferson.

She lay there watching him from the bed for a least seven sentences, pale and nervous-looking with the long illness. Then she cried, "Monty! You didn't—you couldn't—you wouldn't?"

"No!"

"But then who did? Oh, if she couldn't win on her own, you know I'd rather she lost! Why did you—"

"He just told you that he didn't," said her father, rather louder than usual. "Let him go on."

"But if he didn't, it certainly wasn't Beau, and—"

"Julie, I've had enough suspicions thrown at me and

my boys for a year!" Monty snapped. "Please don't *you* start it! Will you let me finish?"

"Go on, son," said Rand, sitting down on the edge of the bed and taking his daughter's hand in a firm grip. "She'll keep quiet."

Monty got through his interview with the steward hastily, and began with the morning paper. It was too much for Julie. "Let me see it! Oh, those *skunks*! But Monty, are you certain that there's nothing to this? After all, what could cloud a test except drugs?"

"Say," Monty grated, badly stung, "what do you think of me, anyway?"

"I think you'd do a lot to make me feel good when I'm all banged up and h-helpless. Maybe even give Bonnie an edge, after she'd been laid off for so long." Tears were cascading down her cheeks.

Monty stood up. His psyche was about as bruised as it could well be. "If you'd rather believe the insinuations of some pinheaded reporter than me, okay. I'll be getting back to Kandahar. I've got to get in touch with Mr. Tolkov about this. Take care of things here, Rand." And before either of them could stop him, Monty was gone, in the grip of further shock, a maimed ego, and a determination never to ask anyone to marry him.

"Well," said Rand. "Time for your medicine, Julie."

"It isn't nearly time."

"Oh yes it is. Doctor's orders. Getting wrought up like this isn't the best thing in the world for your back, you know; you tense your muscles and rattle around in that bed and don't do the poor squoze nerve any good whatever. Here, take this."

"You're going to trank me out of my mind as if I was some skittish filly!" she accused him.

"I'm going to calm you down to human level. Julie," he said, "I haven't had occasion to say it more than two or three times in your whole life, but I'm tempted to tell you now that I'm ashamed of you. The fact that you're partially paralyzed, sick to death of lying in bed, overtired from yesterday's trip, and edgy because you've been away from horses so long, doesn't begin to excuse you for telling Monty he's a liar and a horse-drugger."

"I *never*!"

"Take this." She finally did. "That lad would let himself be trampled to death by mad armadillos for you. He's been a faithful friend to you through years when any horse that jogged past you meant more than he did. He must be feeling now as if this is his ultimate reward for all that devotion, trouble, and dependability: to be suspected of committing an illegal, immoral act upon an animal that he loves as well as you do. Personally, I wouldn't blame him if he took a job training for Jonas Black."

Julie gulped down a large, uncomfortable sob. "I didn't *mean* it that way, Dad. I was just shocked and trying to understand."

"You should have lain here quietly until he'd told you everything about it, instead of leaping in with both feet," said Rand coolly. "Another time, that's what you're to do. That's a royal command. Now relax and let the tranquilizer do its work, Julie. I don't want you back in that hospital with a nervous breakdown."

"No, no, no, I'll be still, I'll be as calm as Pushy. Thanks, Dad."

"You'd chew *me* out for *my* own good, under similar circumstances," said Rand, smiling.

Late that afternoon, Stash and Leon came visiting. They had been eager to see her, but had thought it wise to give her a full day's rest before calling. They both drew their chairs up alongside the bed so that the girl could see and talk to them without having to twist or turn.

Her delight at having them here was obvious. These

two elderly black men had been through a great deal with Julie, adventures and mysteries, catastrophes and equine crises; and their mutual love was so strong that it never had to be mentioned. "I'm so glad you came!" she told them, gripping their hands. "This being nailed down in one place is the absolute worst! Tell me everything about everything—how are the twins? did Dirk get Cache? has Southern Cross foaled yet? how's Pop and Tweedy? how are you?"

"All in good time," said Leon, chuckling deeply. "I see all that hospital rest hasn't slowed up your mental-vocal reflexes any. We'll give you all the news you can listen to, but first we want to hear about you. How you feel, inside and outside, and what the medical dignitaries told you."

"And everything," added Stash.

"Well, I have a whole program of graduated exercises to work on here at home, and the therapist will be over once a week for a while; and I have to go back to the hospital for progress reports every so often, tests and stuff. If things happen as the doctor hopes they will, after while I'll get around as good as ever. If they don't, then it means an operation, but I don't have to think about that for months so I won't. Look at my brand-new crutches over there. Aren't they straight out of a mad doctor's lab? But I'll be gait-walking with them soon." She paused to take a breath.

"And?" said Stash meaningfully.

"And? Oh, *and*. Well, I do get awfully tired doing the exercises. This is the first day I've tried these particular ones, and it isn't quite like working with the therapist, but I'll get the hang of them all right. Dad's a big help. Far's pain goes, it's so much better now than when it happened, I almost don't notice it. Sometimes I forget about hurting for hours, and then it's more like a backache than a real *pain* pain. Now you tell me what's happened here since I saw you last!"

Cross-talking each other, Stash and Leon presented her with a detailed account of farm and horse events, including the news that Dirk had faithfully collected the big jumper Cache on Sunday afternoon, the day after the Marquesa. He'd left word that he was leaving next day for two weeks of showing in Virginia; and that although he wouldn't be entering Cache at either of the two shows, he'd take him along to acquaint him with the atmosphere, and school him over the available courses.

As they continued to answer Julie's questions, the gentle St. Bernard Pushy padded quietly into the room. After acknowledging both of his old buddies with a sedately proffered paw, he folded himself into an unobtrusive mountain of fur at their feet. Soon Barney, now freed of his cast and with only a slight limp, and Percy, the foundling from the racetrack, galloped awkwardly into the bedroom in a lumbering version of follow-the-leader. They had barely crossed the threshhold when Nana stepped forth from her place by the foot of Julie's bed, and with rising hackles and a deep, menacing growl, warned them that this room was off limits for games and rompings. The ungainly young wolfhound and the short-legged mutt sat back on their haunches and bugged their eyes in what seemed actual fear of the threatening beagle.

"Wondered where that little terror was," said Leon. "Thought she'd be out demolishing a paisley shawl or an elm tree. I see she's made herself the guardian of the sickroom."

"I could hardly believe it," said Rand, eyeing the sturdy little dog with affection. "Yesterday, when we'd reached home, the others wanted to run all over the farm—that is, Barney and the pup did. Pushy's such a gent that he all but carried the suitcase into the house.

But Nana, she wasn't having any part of frivolity. She knew that Julie wasn't well, or at least that something was wrong enough so that she wouldn't be playing with the dogs for a while. So, while the youngsters were investigating and Push was being a gentleman, that little beagle went around the house, room to room, gathering her toys. Her rubber bone, that half-chewed rag doll, two old beef bones, numerous balls, a rubber squeaker that long ago gave up its squeak, a bundle of tied-up socks—she kept at it till she had them all assembled on the living-room floor. Then she took them again, one by one, and deposited them behind the overstuffed chair next to the bookcase."

"I'll be doggoned," said Leon quietly.

"After that, Nana took up residence under the foot of Julie's bed, and refuses to leave except to go out once in the morning, once in the afternoon, and once at night. She won't even bark at the others when she's in here: only gives them that low growl. It's really one of the most touching things I've ever seen a dog do."

"The little critter's found some sense at last," said Leon.

"About time she grew up," added Stash, reaching down to scratch the silky brown ears fondly.

Julie said, "I've told you from the very beginning that she's special! Now maybe you'll appreciate how really wonderful she is."

"Seems to me the beagle ain't the only one to go unappreciated around here," mumbled Stash.

"What was that?" asked Julie.

"Uh, I said, uh . . . didn't I see Monty drivin' a car up here?"

"I'm sure that's precisely what you didn't say," said Julie sardonically. Then, changing her tone, "Oh! Since you mention it, has either of you seen the *Herald* today?"

"Yep, I always have reference to a newspaper when I say Monty's name. So, I didn't see it."

"Me neither," said Leon Pitt. "You know we get the *Racin' News* and the Lexington *Post,* which is about all there's time to read in a day. Why'd you ask?"

"Because it says that Bonnie was drugged in the Marquesa!" Julie blurted. With an abrupt rush of words, she told them of the lab report, Monty's summons to the steward's office, and the bold insinuations bordering on libel that appeared in the *Daily Herald.*

Rand gave them the article, and while they scanned it quickly, Julie continued her account, including Monty's short visit.

"So that's why he lit out o' here like a brush fire going someplace to happen," Stash exclaimed. "Never even stopped to say hello."

"Stopped?" said Leon. "Didn't even slow down long enough to wave. And no wonder!"

The two stared at each other a moment. "For the first thing of all," said Stash, "I can't make out how anybody'd have anything to gain by peppin' up Bonnet. There was no way she was gonna pay a big price, after all; so they couldn't have looked to insure a bet."

"And if somebody wanted to get at her, they'd have had to walk over Drop Cord to do it," said Rand. "Four days before the Marquesa, he moved a filly out of the stall next to Bonnie and stuck a cot in there. He slept on it every night, and made sure that someone was under the shed at all times, just on general principles."

"Who could have done it, if it was done?" asked Julie; it was the first time she had speculated aloud on the affair since Monty had gone.

"Who *could?* My boy for one," said Stash. "Monty himself. Drop Cord. And likely any one of the stable crew. Who *didn't?* Beau, Monty, Drop Cord, and all of 'em. That's blame well who didn't."

Rand had been thinking briskly. Now, determined to impress on his daughter's mind once and for all that she must not fly off the handle at old friends without pausing to reflect, and since Stash and Leon were as close to the girl as anyone, he decided to let them help. "The reason that Monty flew out of here like a turpentined hound," he said, "was that Julie thought he might have given Bonnie a slight edge himself."

"Ah, Julie," said Leon sadly.

"Uh-oh!" said Stash. "You went and told Monty that?"

"Yes. And I've been thinking," said Julie, amazing Rand afresh, "and it's just barely possible. You all know that Monty won't let me grow up in his own mind, don't you? I've been sixteen to him for half a dozen years. I can't stand disappointment. A loss for Bonnie would crush me to pulp. No, don't interrupt! He treats me like a porcelain doll with a nervous system made of thread and a jellyfish for a heart. I *know* I get strung up and holler that Bonnie can't lose! But if she did, do any of you believe I'd be smashed to particles?"

"You got a bounce-back constitution that I'd lay a hundred to one on," said Stash instantly.

"But don't you all know perfectly well that Monty's never truly believed that?" she demanded. "Be honest! Why, Leon, you and Stash have even lectured him on it! But he won't see, he won't trust me to handle disappointment! So can you absolutely take your solemn oath cross-your-heart-and-so-on that he wouldn't even give Bonnie a little almost-legitimate supplement of, I don't know, something to move her up? Something that'd make her test cloudy? *Can* you?"

"Yes," said Stash firmly.

Rand nodded. But Leon, after a slight pause, said, "I don't know him as well as you three do, but I do know how much he thinks of Julie . . ."

"No, nope, huh-uh, no way, entirely to the contrary," said Stash.

"Stash! When I was lying in a hospital half paralyzed?"

"Contrariwise," Stash affirmed, pounding fist in palm. "Not even to save you from poverty and woe! Monty's the second most honest man on two feet when it comes to horses!"

"Who's the most, then?" asked Leon suspiciously.

"Me," said Stash. "I say that 'cause I'm inside here, and I know me pretty good."

"Aside from the matter of honesty," said Leon, with a glance sidelong at Stash laden with sarcasm, "let me speak for the young fella, practical and unemotional as compared with some old men I could mention. He'd know as well as any man what would cloud a test. No matter how much he wanted that mare to win, for Julie's sake, and even if he went a little funny in the head wanting it, he would never *ever* risk his license, his lifetime chosen career, Bonnie's terrific record, and the reputation of Deepwater Farm, not for a purse of a million dollars and a miraculous cure for Julie. And that's that."

"Well said," Rand agreed. "Julie, I see how your thinking goes, but Leon's right. It would just be too impractical for Monty to try for a victory in that way."

"The fact that he's an honest soul, that don't enter into your calculations?" Stash said to Leon.

"Course it does! But looked at from the viewpoint of, say, a steward, now: isn't it dumb to think he'd risk all them things even if he was crooked as an eel with the colic?"

"Dumber'n a man who wasn't raised in Ohio," said Stash.

"Look here, *I* wasn't raised in Ohio!"

"No offense meant to present company," said Stash angelically.

"Okay," said Julie, sinking back wearily into the pillows. "You're all right, and I was all wrong. I shouldn't have screeched out my suspicion at Monty, I know that. I ought to have asked him quietly and sweetly if he had any ideas about who might have done it. I'm only sort of bent out of shape, fellows, with not being able to walk or even to ride horses . . . I guess it makes me lame in the head too."

"Nobody's perfect, honey," said Leon. "Except Stash Watkins."

"Even I have a fault or two," said Stash, getting up to leave, "but I'm never gonna confide them to *you*."

Monty Everett had made the return trip to Kandahar Park in record time, forgetting even to stop for gas until he happened to notice that the tank gauge registered below empty. With his mind going up and down on an ebb tide of plots, motivations, possible outcomes, dependable factors and the whole gamut of racing unknowns, the time fled past unnoticed; it seemed that no sooner had he stepped into the car at Fieldstone than he was pulling up at the gates of Kandahar.

In addition to a shadowy solution to the Bonnie crisis that danced tantalizingly just beyond the rim of his consciousness, he could still hear Julie's gasp and see the expression on her face as she accused him: "Monty! You didn't . . . you know I'd rather she lost!" The words slashed him no less with the passage of the hours.

The harder he thought, the more confused he grew. Time and again the situation rose before him from start to finish, and each time he thought he understood, yet found another hole in his reasoning. In the end it was wholly entwined with Julie's cruel reaction, and despite his deep personal hurt he could see the factors contributing to her outburst; unjustified, but understandable.

Now he had exhausted every possible idea on Bonnie's phenomenal win and subsequent lab report. He had a few fairly reasonable notions, and more than a few questions demanding answers. He was out of the car before the engine died, and after a quick look under the shed in Barn 7, which was quiet in the lazy warmth of afternoon, he headed for Drop Cord's room.

"How'd she take it?" was the groom's greeting.

Monty plunked himself down on a chair. "She assumed that I gave Bonnie a boost so that the owner's heart wouldn't be broken."

Drop Cord stared at him. He put down the paper he'd been reading. "You're joking me."

"Not an inch. 'Oh, Monty,' " he said in a falsetto, bitter again, " 'how could you!' "

"You tell her you didn't?"

"Sure. Lot of weight my word carries."

"But you didn't dope that horse!" said Drop Cord vehemently.

"Are you certain?"

The groom blinked twice. "Too right I'm certain."

"Oh. Thanks. Drop Cord, what all's in that tonic you've been giving the mare? I forgot about it when I was talking to Larry."

"What do you mean, what's in it? Haven't we been giving it to every horse under this shed for the past two years? Hasn't every one passed the box without any problems?" Drop Cord bent an eyebrow into a right angle. "I'm not ready to pass on my trade secrets just yet, Monty."

"Absolutely nothing in it that could affect a test, then?"

Drop Cord gazed at him and did not even bother to shake his head.

Monty tried another tack. "Who was in Bonnie's stall, say during the twenty-four hours before the race?"

"Who? *I* was, that's who! Me, 'n' Beau, Marsh, Dan,

you, Mr. Jefferson; and don't forget Dr. Skye, the track vet. He was in there on the morning of the stake to okay her to run. But mainly the trainer. *He* was in there so often, I started to think he'd nominated himself her mascot."

"Are you annoyed at me asking you these questions?" asked Monty, a little surprised.

"You're right on the nailhead I'm annoyed. How could you even suggest such a thing?"

"It's been suggested to me so often lately that I've got to suggest it to every man who works with me in my turn, that's how I can suggest it!" said Monty hotly.

"Sorry, boss. Sorry, sorry, sorry. Never meant to fly off the point of my self-righteousness at you. It's just, you know better, I know better."

"Yeah, we do. Thank heaven for that, anyway."

"Mind you," said Drop Cord suddenly, "to be as fair as I know how, maybe I *would* have moved her up a bit just to be conclusive and absolute that she'd get there first, IF I'd thought there was any way for her to get beat. I'm not sure. I never did it, not ever. But circumstances were rugged, with Julie laid low and all . . . and her legs not getting better . . . I don't know. But I didn't *have* to do anything. That big mare was and is as right as a horse can be; I knew that for fact. I rub that mare. I feed her before I feed myself, and if there had to be a choice 'tween her and me, I don't have to spell out for you who'd go hungry, do I?"

"No."

"I don't sleep till she's settled, and even then I'm back checkin' in the night. I hear every sound she makes all night long. And when it's close to race time, she does the sleeping and I do the watching. I live with that mare and I know her good's I know my own self. When I told you she'd win, that was no casual promise! I can spot a fit horse when I see one, and 'class' is so rare you can't miss it. No sir," said Drop Cord loudly, "Bonnie don't need a thing to improve her performance on the oval! She's all run and heart—"

"You don't have to sell me, I'm on her team too."

"And I'll tell you another thing," said the groom, shaking an enormous finger under Monty's nose, "she's fixed and ready to whip the next field she meets, whoever's in it!"

Monty nodded. "I admire enthusiasm, Drop Cord, but how can you be so positive that she'll win again and again when you don't even know what they'll be running at her? No one can be that dogmatic without a reason."

"I prefer to think of it as horsematic," said Drop Cord. "Now don't you feel the same way about Bonnie?"

"Not to that fanatical an extent. There are other great horses in the world."

"Son," said the groom gently, "I'm a lot older around tracks than you are. I've seen racehorses come and go down the years, and I've worked on some of the best. Dr. Lejeune traveled all over this land, and even to Europe a few times, treatin' the immortals of the turf. I was with him a long time, and had the privilege of handlin' over twenty of the greatest. Horses that set records and made history. Horses that were legends in their time, horses that got to be legends accounta their offspring. That kind of horses got a special way about them. Some call it 'the look of eagles.' I like that. Or can you call it heart, or class, whatever you want, but if you've seen it once, you never miss it when it's there. Bonnie has it all. *And* the generosity to give till there's nothing left."

"That's true."

"Okay: now I know every mare that might even think about trying to run with her. Of a possible thirty, let's say, at least half will simply avoid the challenge by running somewhere else. You want me to name 'em, I can.

Why should they hook up with her and get whipped, when all those other purses are available at the same time, and theirs for the taking? Of the other fifteen, six have already tried her and lost; and I bet no more'n two of them try to run with her again. Leaving nine who'll try for sure. I've figured them, I know for a fact that not one of them can catch her. If Bonnie gets left, it'll be an accident or a fluke, and you don't take them things into consideration when you're sayin' that your horse can beat anything under a saddle! And even if racing luck deserts her, she's never gonna be no piece of cake!"

Monty stood up. "It's part of either my trade or my nature," he said, "not to be quite as optimistic as you. But I'm glad that you feel the way you do, man. It eases my mind, for no reason I can think of." He laughed shortly. "The test did come back cloudy. The steward did warn me. The owner did say I was suspected of being a no-good bum. Nevertheless, Drop Cord, listening to you on the matter of Bonnie, I feel weirdly relieved! Thanks."

"Any time, chief. Just don't go to supposin' again, in my presence, that I might be giving that big girl anything illegal. Or," finished the groom, standing too, so that he towered over the trainer, "I wouldn't say absolutely that I wouldn't throw away my job for the joy of dropping you into a mud puddle."

They shook hands, grinning.

There was a third prime suspect, and Monty knew as well as he knew any fact in this world that Stash's son would die rather than drug a horse, but he felt it necessary to do at least some sketchy sleuthing in that direction; so next morning, before the working day began and the horses started going out on the track, he collared Beau. The jockey saw through his clumsy suggestions and was obviously annoyed.

"You asked Drop Cord about this in private yet?"

"I did. But I didn't really suspect him any more than I do you," said Monty sadly. "I just don't *know* anything."

"I would hope you'd know me better'n that by now," said Beau, just as mournful. "I wouldn't give a horse anything ever! I got to ride those horses. It's my neck out there, and I want the sharpest, most alertest animal under me that I can find. I want him in control of all his senses, not under the influence of some drug or other. A drugged horse to me is worse than a drunk jock! And if I wasn't riding, I still wouldn't be anywhere on the dopin' bit. My father would die of shame if I let such a thought into my skull, and you know how much I love Dad. And I don't hate any jock bad enough to see him up on a horse that isn't perfectly normal. That answer your worries?"

"I wish it did. There aren't any answers that we can find, I feel it, Beau. You know I wouldn't distrust you if I found you with a hypodermic needle in your hand."

"Listen, Monty," said the small man kindly, "if anyone can tell you that she wasn't drugged, I can. I could no more have stopped that mare out there than—well, than hold back an elephant from a hay bale with a rope of cobwebs. She ran her own race and was nice enough to let me go along for the ride. But she ran it her way, Bonnie's way, and if that hadn't been one hundred percent Bonnie under me, I'da sensed it, you know?"

"You would for sure. I don't understand it at all."

"I heard a word or two before that test came back," said Beau, "about how maybe the Marquesa was a boat race." This is a racetrack term for a fixed race, in which the jockeys have agreed among themselves to pull their horses so that a horse, usually the one with the longest odds, can win, all the riders having bet on that beast. "But you don't need telling that it was straight."

"I don't. Neither, I'm sure, does Mr. T. It's only that blasted test."

"The other boys would have loved to beat her," Beau plunged on. "I know for a fact that the boy on Ruby Frump had bet a bundle on her 'cause he figured she'd up and take to running. Besides, what would they—or *I* —have gained by lettin' Bonnie win by such an all-fired silly big margin like that? All we'd have gotten would be nice long suspensions. Right?"

"Affirmative. There's only one thing I'd like to know, for the record: when you left us at the barn that morning, you said you had a little errand to run before reporting to the Jock's Room. Would you mind telling me what sort of errand that was?"

Beau squinted at him. After a lengthy pause he said, "I don't really want to tell you now, Monty."

"Later?"

"Promise."

"Okay." Monty went off to his duties, no wiser than he'd been twenty-four hours ago.

A moment later Drop Cord materialized at Beau's side. The jockey jumped. "Man! You come on like a dinosaur outa the woodwork! Can't you make a little racket with your feet? Scare a guy out of his bridgework."

"You're skittish and fidgety today, aren't you? Monty been grillin' you?"

"Well, he has to. He knows better, but it's his job."

"*Do* you know anything about it, Beau?"

"D.C.," said Beau fiercely, "if one more person, identity unspecified, asks me anything about drugging racers, or for that matter brood mares or burros or jackasses, I'm gonna reach way up and sock that person on the shinbone!"

"Little fella," said Drop Cord solemnly, "we have to get to the bottom of it. You consider, all things taken into account, it could have been anyone in the universe except one of us three?"

"What, you 'n' me 'n' Monty Everett?"

"They're the trio I meant."

"Well, how you like this back at you?" said Beau in a fury. "Do you honest-and-true think it *was* one of us?"

Drop Cord rubbed his chin. "Can't say I do. Not way down inside where it counts."

"Then let's use our gourds for a change. Who hates Monty enough to fix his horse for him? 'Cause it couldn't be somebody gettin' back at any of the rest of us—it's Monty's responsibility. You know anyone would want him out of the way?"

"No," said Beau slowly. "Least, nobody but some old crooks that ain't been seen near a track in years. And they'd have to lay out money to have it done, or risk more jail by doin' it themselves, and I doubt they hate him that bad. They're in the past. No, I discount anybody on the outside."

"Can't do that unless it's one of us. What about that Markham character? Anybody with one bad eye can see he's crazy about Julie."

"So he drugs her horse for her. No, he's out. Leon Pitt and my dad swear by him. When he fights Monty, it'll be clean."

"All right, I'll take your pop's word. Let's go talk to Monty."

"What for? None of us knows anything!"

Drop Cord put a hand on his shoulder. "We can at least tell one another that none of us suspects one of us."

"Yeah. If I understand that sentence, you're right. We got to hang together," said Beau gloomily, "through whatever can be coming next. I got a miserable feeling it won't be a package of delirious fun."

"We've had one calamity," agreed Drop Cord, "and

there's bound to be two more on the way. Always threes. I never saw it fail. Threes."

"Try not to be so cheerful. It makes my teeth hurt," said Beau. They trailed away to find Monty.

Chapter TEN

In the eleven days that remained until the Dresden Handicap, Julie made marvelous progress, despite the fact that the days were far too short to accommodate all the practice and therapy that she wanted to cram into them. Rand was repeatedly warning her to ease off a bit, and not to overdo her exercises, but she was unshakable in her determination to attend Bonnie's next race on her own two feet, albeit with the aid of her new crutches. Her dedication and singlemindedness, plus her father's occasional firm commands, paid off handsomely: her doctor allowed her to begin with the shiny metal supports a full six days before the race. Spurred on by this, Julie worked at mastering her crutch coordination to the limit of her strength, and though she still tired easily, was relatively sure of her ability to get around safely with a day and a half to spare.

When she was not concentrating on moving her intractable legs by sheer force of will, she more often than not was thinking hard and long about the peculiar circumstances surrounding Bonnie's lab report, so that these two matters took up the greater part of her attention. Even though she suffered much anxiety over the mare problem, Rand Jefferson was grateful for the diversion of it, because it kept her from dwelling exclusively on the fact that in spite of her exemplary performance on the crutches, there was really not much improvement in her ability to move about on her own. Naturally he did not mention his increasing fear, and scolded himself for his lack of patience: the prognosis had been based on *time,* yet here he was, rushing things as impetuously as Julie herself. So he would over-compensate for his thoughts, and lecture his daughter on her relentless drive to recover.

Unlike Julie's days, which seemed sadly inadequate, Monty Everett felt each leaden hour crawling past him, and sometimes wondered if the day would end at all. He still smarted from Julie's outburst, and although she had apologized the next evening when he called, he couldn't utterly forget the hurt: he'd confined his conversation to a brief summary of the happenings in Barn 7, which was about as personal as, and in fact closely resembled, a weather report. The subsequent calls were not much better as he sank further into a dismayed gloom; while he would not admit it, he viewed the upcoming race with dreadfully conflicting emotions. On the one hand, he longed for the time to fly by so that he could soon run the mare and clear his reputation; on the other, he was genuinely fearful that the "unknown factor" would produce the same results . . . even though his inclination was to regard the thing as an inexplicable fluke.

Certain that no one in Deepwater's employ was responsible for that semi-positive test, and doubtful that anyone from beyond their circle could get at the mare past Drop Cord, Beau, Marsh, and himself, he nevertheless hired three independent (that is, not from the track) security guards from the Whitney Agency, and arranged to place Bonnie under twenty-four-hour surveillance for the week preceding the Dresden.

Once again the mare trained brilliantly. The highlight was a black-letter work: this is the fastest work for every distance each day, which appears in black type next day in the *Racing Form,* as long as it was recorded by the official track clockers. This particular one left the clockers mumbling to themselves and sent two trainers to the office to scratch their tentative starters from the line-up for the Dresden. As Drop Cord had predicted, there were enough big-money races available across the country so that, unless a trainer believed that his horse had a very fair chance of beating Bonnie for the lion's share of the purse, he saw no need to confront her at all.

Even Monty had to admit aloud that Bonnie was the horse to beat; although his conservative nature required him to follow that with mental and verbal allowances for the anything-can-happen quality of horse racing, for the possibility of an off track (a track that is rated anywhere less than "fast"), and for the possibility that the concession of six to fifteen pounds among the rest of the field might reduce her chances to something less than odds-on favorite.

Just as staunchly as before, Drop Cord and Beau held that Bonnie would annihilate the competition, but with the recent near-disaster so fresh in their minds, they forbore to mention this to Monty when he'd finished listing his if's and but's and however's. As they walked away together, Beau clucked his tongue sympathetically. "Poor Monty, he doesn't dare let out his enthusiasm. He's got it, but I think he's superstitious about it! He's that way with Julie all the time—my dad says, he's all the time discounting her chickens before they're hatched."

Drop Cord laughed. "Your dad's got a nice touch with the words there. That's Monty all right."

The young trainer himself was at the same moment thinking heavily on the same subject. It had occurred to him with increasing frequency lately that what he'd always thought of as Julie's insane optimism had produced in him a kind of insane pessimism. Of the two, if you must have one, he thought, it's certainly better to err on the happy side. He resolved not to inflict his but's, still's, yet's, and however's on anyone again.

However ridiculously they anticipated the best possible outcome only!

On race day, Julie and Rand left the farm early, to have plenty of time both for traveling and for a quick visit to the stable area before the running of the Dresden. Rand hoped that all this, in combination with the overwhelming excitement of the race, would not prove too much for the girl. Yet she was so eager to demonstrate her skill with the crutches, and had worked so very hard, that he hadn't the heart to deny her any part of her schedule. So they reached Kandahar and went to Barn 7.

The crew were delighted to see her up and around again, even if she was leaning heavily on the artificial aids. Above their mingled voices, Bonnie split the stable air with a high sharp whinny of joyous welcome. Monty hovered beside Julie as she slowly made her way toward her beloved mare's stall. He had the urge to lift and carry her down the aisle, but, summoning his insight, realized that it would be a happier day for Julie if she managed to accomplish as much as possible on her own. When she had been nuzzled and butted and slurped at by the overjoyed Bonnie, she turned and deliberately fell into Monty's arms.

"Have you forgiven me?"

"Of course I have," said Monty. "Have you decided that I'm innocent of evil where horses and drugs are concerned?"

"I never suspected you! I only sounded like it. Have you realized that Bonnie's going to win again?"

"In a walk. By unimaginable lengths," said Monty blithely.

"Wonders never cease, do they?" said Drop Cord to Beau.

Then Mr. T himself, twinkly of eye, bristly of beard, and rotund of paunch, entered the stable, radiating anticipation. "Another seventeen-length win?" he called to Monty. "A new track record today?" His gaze passed over the three uniformed guards, who were watching everyone narrowly. "Ah, good thinking," he said to Monty.

"Thank you, sir." The trainer glanced around. "The gang's all here, all right—guess it's just as well to have three pairs of strange eyes on the lookout, considering."

"Right, my boy."

"Dirk isn't here," said Rand innocently.

"I wish he could have been," said Julie. "But he called last night, Monty, and he's so pleased with Cache that he's going to ride him, for the first time, in competition. Isn't that marvelous?"

"Superbly wonderful," said Monty in a deliberately dull tone.

"Don't be like that," said Julie. "Just because Cache isn't a racing horse!"

Monty turned slightly red in the face, and Rand hastily walked out of the barn so he could laugh freely.

The light on the tote board indicated that the track condition was fast. As if in defiance of the handicapper's effort to create an equal field by means of the weight assignments, Bonnie pranced and played her way onto the track while leading the post parade as the number one horse. Beau was hard put to keep her in hand, galloping beside the pony during the warm-up; and for the first time in her racing career, an assistant starter was told to stand by her head in the gate while the other eight horses were loaded. With the inside post position the race strategy was relatively simple, provided that they encountered no special problems. Bonnie was fast out of the gate, so there would be no trouble establishing a good position on the rail. If any horse or horses looked as though they wanted to set the pace and "run on the Bill Daley"—that is, stay in front all the way and lead wire to wire—then Beau would let them fight it out among themselves while he sat neatly in the number two, three, or even four spot till they rounded the final turn at the top of the stretch.

At that point he would let her begin to move, and unless the Deepwater trio were mistaken in their over-all evaluation of the opposition, Bonnie would overtake the leaders and outrun any possible challengers from behind. If no one moved up to take the lead within the first quarter of a mile, then Beau would have to set the pace, trying to keep the big mare in check and rate her only as fast as those behind forced her to go in order to maintain her position.

Monty preferred to let her come from slightly off the pace; but Beau was certain that no matter which way it worked out, Bonnie would be more than capable of handling the situation. "Fact is," he'd confided to Monty as the horses were being saddled in the paddock, "I'd almost *like* to break on top and just let 'em try to catch us! Why, we'd put away at least four of 'em before the half, another two by the quarter, and if the last pair still thought they wanted to run with us for another quarter of a mile, all I can say's they'd have to catch us first! And they couldn't!"

"Certainly hope you aren't gonna get lonesome out there all by yourself," Drop Cord had grinned at him. As the paddock judge called "Riders up," Beau had

settled lightly on top of the tiny racing saddle and said,
"Bonnie is all the company I need!"

Now the number one post position has only one
drawback. Unless there is some special reason and the
trainer arranges for the change beforehand, number one
is the first horse in the gate and must stand there until
all the animals are loaded and ready to break. This
means that a nervous horse may fret and chafe with excitement and therefore be unprepared at the start, or
fidget himself into a poor stance or an unbalanced carriage, thus delaying his getaway. It also means that a
sleepy horse may become bored with waiting and allow
himself to lose the fine edge of alertness that's needed if
he is to spring from the gate the instant the doors fly
open.

So, if there are undue delays in assembling all the
horses in the gate, the early horses may have to be taken
out and reloaded. Efforts are made to avoid this situa-
ton, and often an assistant starter will steady the first
animal's head and try to keep it in the stall and ready to
run. This was the case with Bonnie as she stamped and
snorted in her impatience to be off and running in the
Dresden.

She was not quite straight as they finally maneuvered
the number six horse into position and hustled the re-
maining three to their posts in record time. Consequent-
ly, when the starter sprung the latch, she was ill-pre-
pared to break. Her reflexes were so conditioned to
spring forward when the bells rang and the doors
opened that she left the gate anyway. Instantly she stumbled and almost fell to her knees. Beau was snatched
rudely forward as the reins ripped through his hands
with the down-thrust of her head. Miraculously, she
managed to stay on her feet, and Beau was snapped
back into a semblance of the proper position on her

back, though the reins were nearly out of his reach on her neck.

The crowd gave a sort of great grunting sigh of sympathy and Julie stifled a small cry as her mare lurched out of the gate; then she watched wide-eyed as Bonnie regained solid footing and reached her stride some four lengths behind the tightly bunching field.

"Good-bye game plan," growled Monty.

"What do you mean?" said Julie.

"I mean Beau can't possibly race her with the reins in a mess like that, and just look at her!"

Julie hadn't removed her gaze from Bonnie since she'd set foot on the track, and certainly didn't need to be ordered to watch her. With increasing awe she saw the great mare lengthen her already gigantic stride as the field headed into the first turn. The mare hugged the rail as she made the turn herself, gaining ground with every stride. They emerged from this turn slightly strung out, with Bonnie no more than a length behind the last horse and no more than ten lengths separating her from the leader.

Beau was trying to regain control, but his near fall and lost reins gave Bonnie the freedom she wanted; without hesitation she aimed for the outside of the pack, passing all but the leaders within the next quarter-mile. Although there was a comfortable three-quarters of a mile still to go, she picked off the leaders briskly, and ran with what looked like the barest of efforts into the stretch, showing the others her heels by a comfortable three-length margin.

Every human soul was afoot now, even Julie was up as tall as she could manage on her crutches. The park was one gargantuan roar of sound. The girl, shrieking herself, was aware of two voices on either side of her: Rand howling the mare's name over and over, and Mr. Tolkov bellowing, *"The finest horse in the world!"*

As they moved into the final quarter, a short-striding and powerful roan made a gallant bid to challenge her. As if to emphasize the almost contemptuous ease with which she ran, and the extent of the handicapper's error in estimating her condition and ability, Bonnie surged ahead in a blinding explosion of speed and shot across the finish line a dozen lengths in advance of her nearest rival.

The crowd gave a splendid imitation of a vast roll of thunder. There was no longer any doubt that at least one horse had come back from an injury as capable as, if not more capable than she had been before it, and everyone there seemed to be cheering her success.

The Deepwater contingent headed in an ecstatic, babbling knot to the winner's circle. Julie spoke for them all when she exclaimed, "Now let them claim she was doped! Nobody's been near her and nothing's been different from last time—she won fair and square and on her own, and they can't take that away from her!"

Monty grinned at her indignation and the open challenge in her voice to any who would criticize her equine star. For the first time since that report had come back from the lab after the Marquesa, he was able to accomplish something resembling relaxation. Here he'd seen the vindication that he'd sought. On the way to the stable, he even exchanged quips with a friend who made a joking reference to the race-before-last, not realizing how much Monty had suffered because of the suspicion.

Drop Cord summed it up later that afternoon as he carefully wrapped Bonnie's legs and took a final swipe at her gleaming hide. "Whatever happened before has got to be a freak, some fool accident in a test tube. No way, *none,* can that box be positive or even cloudy this time, and we all know nothin's different. I don't guess they'll ever apologize, boss," he added, knowing well the extent of Monty's pain, "but it'll make you feel fine just makin' them recognize they were at fault."

"Yes. Thanks. If—" said Monty slowly, feeling a cold breeze along his spine, "if they were."

"Has to be that way," said the groom positively.

Forty-seven hours and ten minutes later, Monty remembered those words as he stood once again in Larry O'Neill's spartan office and faced the older man squarely across the cluttered desk top.

"Positive? How can it be? Never mind how, it simply *can't* be! Larry, there has to be some mistake, some horrible mistake. I tell you that nobody has been near that mare. Me, my stable foreman, my jock, her owner for a couple of minutes—no one else. The Whitney guards never stepped inside the stall, and no other member of the crew went anywhere near her; not even my assistant trainer, Gibson!"

Larry sighed, looking a little haggard. "Monty, I not only appreciate your position, I feel as if this was happening to me. But there isn't a single thing I can do. Rules are rules. This is a dead-serious offense. If we were to excuse every trainer who yelled 'frame,' 'mistake,' or 'impossible,' racing'ld be wide open for every dude that wanted to hop a horse to win or tranquilize him to quit. We try our hardest to keep it clean for the betting public. They're our bread and butter, and if they can't count on a fair performance and believe the form they read, then they'll find something else to bet on—the dogs, or football, or lotteries—and racing will be as extinct as the brontosaurus."

"Larry, can you honestly say that you think I'd do such a thing?"

O'Neill shook his head slowly.

"Well, then—"

"It was done."

"With Sunbonnet and all that money at stake, not to

mention my reputation, my career, would I take a chance at losing all that just to cash a bet? Come on, old friend! It'd make more sense if she'd lost. Ran out of the money. At least then you could imagine I'd been holding her so a long shot could win. What could I *gain* from hopping Sunbonnet?"

"Ten percent of a big purse that she might not have been able to win otherwise, for one thing," said the steward mildly. "I don't believe it, son, but you've got to look at the possibilities."

"A-a-ahh! Nobody went near that mare!" Monty interrupted, fairly shouting as the flush of anger rose quickly to his hairline.

The steward's voice acquired a definite edge. "Look, a trainer is responsible for his horse under all conditions, and that's that! I'd like to believe you without a trace of doubt—as a personal friend, I do, at least where *your* connivance is concerned—but a cloudy test out of the Marquesa followed by a positive for amphetamine after the Dresden . . . well, let's say that the Kentucky State Racing Commission doesn't appreciate being played for fools, and that my private opinion of Monty Everett isn't worth a horsehair in the soup."

"I don't know what's going on," said Monty, plaintive, overcome abruptly by the gravity of the thing, "but that mare's in the best form of her life. She's training like something unreal! She improves every time she sets hoof to track. I don't need anything artificial to make her run!"

O'Neill folded his hands, avoiding the pleading expression on Monty's distraught face. "On the basis of this positive report," he said formally, "I must tell you that the mare Sunbonnet will be suspended from racing at this meeting pending her transfer to another trainer who's acceptable to the Board of Stewards. You, as her trainer, will be suspended indefinitely, and the charge will be referred at once to the Racing Commission for a hearing. You will naturally be denied all privileges of the grounds until the suspension is settled and served. And my own view, which is that you're the victim of some plot that's too subtle or crazy for me to fathom, doesn't matter an iota."

"You can't mean it."

"I'm afraid I do."

Silently he turned and left the room. Stunned, angry, bewildered, he returned to the barn to tell Dan and the men of this shattering development. In wide-eyed still-ness they gathered about him and listened.

"I'll ask Katie Lyle if she'll take over on Bonnie. I know the stewards will approve of her. I'll see if she can stay under this shed or if Drop Cord can go with her, or something." His voice trailed off.

"You mean you're gonna sit still and let 'em hang you?" It was the practical-minded Beau. "Not even gon-na fight back?"

"What do you suggest I do?" Monty was suddenly sick of the whole business. It was too unfair to believe.

"Have your attorney file the papers to keep 'em from redistributin' the purse, for starters! Then let's figure if there isn't some way to prove what's wrong. Whatever you do, you can't give up. Not when we all know that Bonnie ran on her own."

"The test says she didn't. They could hardly be wrong twice with the same horse." His voice was like lead.

"I sat on a doped colt once, before I came with Tol-kov," Beau persisted. "I didn't know it, but I did know something wasn't kosher. Bonnie was all herself."

Drop Cord said emphatically, "The boy's right. Get hold of your lawyer and ask for a check on the lab pro-cedures. Anything to keep 'em from redistributing that purse, for just as long as you can."

Monty nodded. "I guess that's right. I'm going to call

Mr. T—only I can't imagine how I'll explain what I can't fathom myself." He took a long breath. "I'll stop by Katie's shed on my way out. Take care of things, Dan, D.C., all of you. Lord knows how long it'll take, but we'll get things straight. I'm sure you'll do fine."

"Wow," said Drop Cord quietly, as Monty departed. "I just remembered: this is number two. What's the third misfortune, and when's it set to strike?"

Katherine Lyle listened soberly as Monty explained himself and asked whether she would be willing to saddle Bonnie and assume the responsibility of being her temporary trainer. "Drop Cord knows her as well as I do. I've had my eye on the Milford Cup, three weeks from Wednesday. I've more or less worked out the schedule for Bonnie, so it's just the formality of your accepting."

Katie said, "No chance that someone under your shed had anything to do with these mind-bending wins and the tests? You know I believe in *you,* and if you vouch for them I'll believe that too. But if there's the slightest doubt . . . well, it can mean my license out the window right along with yours, and I can't afford that, Monty."

"I swear everybody in Barn 7 is above suspicion, Katie, and somehow I'm going to prove it. I'd never take advantage of your faith in me, or risk your license if I thought there was any hanky-panky from my boys."

"Okay. Shake hands with Sunbonnet's new trainer. Provided the stewards approve of me."

"Thanks, Katie," said Monty fervently. "Thanks more than I can say. You won't be sorry."

Unable to reach Mr. Tolkov personally, Monty left a short, harried message with a secretary and asked that the magnate return his call as soon as possible. Less than four hours later, Monty opened the door of his efficiency apartment near the racetrack to discover Mr. T standing there at the peak of a purple rage.

"What's going ON!" The normally jovial gentleman strode in, wakening echoes that Monty had never heard there before. "Has every one of you gone mad?"

"Hello, sir," Monty choked in surprise. "I didn't know you were coming. I could have—"

"Could have left a reasonable message with Jenny, instead of a garble of nonsense about suspensions, new trainers, and amphetamine! I was on my way to Fieldstone, and I turned around and set down here instead. Called O'Neill when I arrived. He told me. What *happened?*"

With numerous interruptions from the agitated, pacing owner, Monty explained about everything as well as he could. Gradually Mr. T's anger simmered down into perplexity. "Monty," he said at last, "my trust in you isn't broken, not by a long shot. I'd as soon theorize that Julie slipped her mare a pill. You know that."

Monty thanked him gratefully. "I didn't know it," he said. "At this moment, I don't know anything except that it's three o'clock in the afternoon. And I'm not positive that my watch is right."

"We're faced with a baffling, apparently impossible situation. I can't conceive what the answer will be. But we'll find it. Oh, and incidentally," said Mr. T, with a shadow of his customary twinkle, "your watch *is* wrong. It's two thirty-six."

Monty groaned. It was the next-to-last straw, and he could feel his back bending, ready to snap under one more nightmare wisp.

"You talked to your lawyer?" asked Tolkov.

"Yes, he's putting the legal procedures in motion to stop the redistribution of the Dresden purse. Unless," said the young man gloomily, and without a trace of humor, "he had a heart attack as he was picking up the phone to do it." He took off his watch and wound it; it had run down almost twelve hours before. "I *think* that my name's Montgomery Everett," he mumbled, "although you could argue me out of that, too."

"Come on, son, it's always darkest before the dawn."

"And every cloud has a silver plate in its head, ready to fall on you if you get optimistic," said Monty.

"You and I are going straight to Larry O'Neill," said Mr. T firmly, "and you aren't to forget for a second that I'm behind you."

A little heartened, Monty followed him as he rolled off toward the track.

After a sentence or two of courteous greeting, Mr. T came to the point. "I realize your position, Larry," he said reasonably. "However, you must admit that it would be insanity, sheer raving insanity, to drug the same horse twice in a row. Not to mention the fact that the horse is Sunbonnet. Now: suppose you call in the stable foreman, the jockey, and the Whitney guards, and ask them to sign statements or affidavits or whatever you require. We'll sit here until *something* is settled." He adjusted his flawless tie and settled firmly into a chair, looking like Authority incarnate.

It took the best part of three hours to round up Beau, Drop Cord, and the three Whitney guards, record and transcribe their statements, and have these signed and witnessed. Each man testified independently that to his knowledge, no unauthorized persons had entered the stall, and further swore that he had administered no forbidden substance to the mare. During most of this time, Monty and Mr. T were buried in earnest conversation in a corner of the room.

When all five papers were on the steward's desk, Rollin Tolkov stood up and began to speak very formally.

"You now have before you the sworn statements of five different persons—six, if you count Monty Everett's, which he'll give you any time you desire it—declaring the innocence of themselves as well as one another. Three of these deponents are outsiders: that is, not in the regular employ of Deepwater Farm. I think that ought to count for something.

"I'd like to propose a plan, which, though a shade irregular, I want you to consider. It should clear this matter once and for all."

"Go ahead, Rollin. You know we'd much rather be wrong than right in this case. What's your idea?"

"Monty tells me there's another race for Sunbonnet in three weeks. The Milford Cup. I want to move her from our barn into a kind of quarantine situation, in a stall of your choice in the stakes barn. I'll be glad to pay for the hiring of round-the-clock guards, selected by the track, to maintain twenty-four-hour surveillance. These guards will take all feed and water to the mare, accompany her at all times to and from the track, walk with her hot-walker, and oversee her every move.

"Katie Lyle has agreed to saddle her for the Milford and take the responsibility for her training.

"Of course, under such circumstances there cannot possibly be a positive return on the test from the Milford. If the mare runs the same style of race that she ran in the Marquesa and the Dresden, then I think you'll have to weigh the evidence with extreme care in the judgment of the charges against Monty, and perhaps look into the laboratory procedures and just how stringently they're followed."

Larry O'Neill glanced at his watch. "It's after six, Rollin, and the other stewards have gone for the day. What you're asking is highly irregular—"

"Yet, given the factors we're dealing with, not unreasonable."

"Right," said Larry. "I'm in no position to make such a decision alone, though. I'll take it up with the rest of the board in the morning, and let you know. I can't make any promises."

"That's good enough for me," said Mr. T. "I'll call you in the morning. Early."

"And if we're still quarreling about it, I'll call you back," said Larry, looking rather used up.

Next day Larry received three calls from Deepwater's owner, beginning at nine fifteen and spaced out at quarter-hour intervals. To the last one he answered, in a mood of mixed triumph and worry, "You're in, Rollin. There was a genuine hassle over it, worse than I'd anticipated, and all three of us are still reluctant because it's such a blasted unusual request, but it'll be done the way you want it. I stuck my neck out for you," he said frankly, "and I hope you're right about this. What swung it finally was your reputation, in both the racing and the business worlds, and not Monty's. Don't tell him that, though; the poor guy's wretched enough."

"Thanks, Larry," said Mr. T. "You watch, this is going to clear it all up."

"I hope so," said Larry O'Neill. "We'll now proceed with your plan."

"It will work," said Mr. T as jauntily as possible. "It *has* to work."

Chapter *ELEVEN*

That day the necessary guards were selected and posted, and Bonnie herself was exiled to the stakes barn. None of her own people except Drop Cord and Beau were permitted to go near her new quarters. Bonnie objected shrilly and frequently to the move, especially when she discovered that there were no other residents in this special barn at the time of her settling in there. The stakes barn is reserved for incoming stakes competitors who are not stabled at Kandahar, but have shipped in for a specific race; such contenders arrive from two days to a week before a major event, so that the small structure is in effect a hotel for an elite group of transients. Bonnie plainly felt lost and abandoned in the place, until enough visits from her rider and groom, as well as a progressive familiarity with the sight of the guards, accustomed her to it.

Monty's hearing was conducted on the basis of the existing, provable evidence—the positive results of the lab test—and despite his protestations of innocence and the statements of his crew and the Whitney men, the Racing Commission set him down for sixty days. The action on redistribution of the purse was still pending, and the money had been placed by the racetrack in an escrow account to earn interest until the case could be heard and decided in a court of law.

Because he would not be allowed on the grounds of any track, Monty returned to Deepwater Farm to sit out his sentence. He was only thirty miles from Kandahar, near enough, he thought, to get there fast in an emergency (although what he would do there, being barred from the place itself, never entered his head). Daily he talked on the phone with Drop Cord and Dan Gibson about Bonnie and his other charges. He did not go to Fieldstone to see Julie, for he could not face the prospect of talking about his unearned disgrace to anyone else at any length, though they kept in touch by telephone.

For Julie, it was a horrible period of time; by now she realized that Monty could not have had the remotest hand in Bonnie's betrayal, and she would not credit the notion that Beau or any other friend of hers might have done it for any reason under the clear blue sky. It remained a hideous mystery without a satisfactory answer.

She had become an expert on the metal crutches, but notwithstanding the nearly eight weeks that had elapsed, during which she had gained back most of her control over her body, there was still pressure on the nerve and she had no independent walking ability whatever. With the crutches she was all right; without them, helpless. Her doctor was now glancing at the advisability of an operation; the thought frightened her, but less than the chance of a lifetime without walking freely . . . or riding.

Bonnie, naturally, took a large portion of her thoughts too: if Something or Someone Unknown had "got at her" before, Julie reasoned, past all her devoted guardians, then It or He could do it again.

Bonnie, Monty, motor nerves—add to these the halt in her plans for that longed-for animal shelter, and the possibility that with Bonnie's winnings tied up, the whole grand plan might never come to fruition—Julie Jefferson had never had such a protracted siege of dejection in her life!

Once again, however, the weather smiled broadly for the entire week before the running of the Milford Cup, rendering the track lightning fast on race day. Bonnie was in prime condition as Drop Cord led her into the paddock beneath the shade of the stately oak trees, and Katie Lyle met Mr. T with a grin as she saddled Bonnie, who, because of her overwhelming victories in the last two races, had become the reigning darling of the turf. As Katie lifted Beau into the saddle, there was no last-minute joking, though, and only the girl smiled; the tension of the three men was almost tangible.

When the horses moved onto the track, Katie accompanied Mr. T to his box, where they joined Julie and Rand. Looking at the expressions of the three grave people beside her, she wished for a second or two that the big mare wouldn't even be on the board. Yet this fancy was swiftly reversed as Katie realized that a loss would merely intensify the problem, and that their only redemption would come from a decisive victory followed by a negative test. She believed in these people, and had backed her faith by laying her own career on the line. Even with the peculiar sanction of the stewards, she was still taking the responsibility for the mare by saddling her.

"I hope she wins by a country mile!" she said to herself. "And if she does, I'll take her to the box myself!"

The running of the Milford Cup was practically a rerun of the Marquesa, save that the time for the race only equaled the existing track record, that Bonnie's margin at the finish was closer to ten lengths than seventeen, and that in the nine-horse field strung out behind her were four well-beaten male horses, who had been harder for her to distance than the other mares.

When Bonnie crossed the finish line alone, Katie Lyle emitted an exultant war whoop, and as if it had been a signal, the occupants of the box were suddenly laughing and chattering around her. Julie Jefferson was up and away on her crutches, heading for the winner's circle to greet her gallant mare, while Rand and Mr. T exchanged smiles and exclamations on the brilliant race Bonnie had run and the reconsideration of Monty's suspension that it should effect.

"Certainly they'll find some defect in the chemicals, or the screening system, or—well, something like that," said Rand. "We'll likely never know just what went wrong, but it's obvious that she won as easily this time as she did the others. And we know how this test will read."

On Friday morning a group of people assembled in the large outer office in the administration building at Kandahar Park. Monty Everett had arrived at a summons from the Racing Commission; Julie and her father had come from Deepwater, where they had stayed after the Milford, anxiously awaiting the news from the lab; Rollin Tolkov had previously arranged his schedule so that he could be at Kandahar that morning; and Katie Lyle was there by order of the stewards.

All three of these men were present, and, somewhat ominously, the members of the board of the State Racing Commission. When Larry O'Neill spoke, his voice carried a peculiar tone. "I hardly know how to begin."

"Just begin," said Julie audibly; she was strung up to a painful pitch by all the unsmiling officialdom.

"It seems that the laboratory reports a positive test for amphetamine on the mare Sunbonnet."

"What!" It was Julie's voice that dominated, though all five of them had said it.

"In view of the unusual circumstances surrounding this horse, and the extensive precautions that were taken to ensure that no outside persons had any contact with her, we can only rule that the mare Sunbonnet be suspended from racing until a satisfactory explanation can be found," said Larry.

He turned to Katie Lyle in the terrible hush that followed those words. "Mr. Tolkov has assured us of your innocence, Miss Lyle, and because of the unique situation, we don't feel that you ought to be suspended, though you certainly risked it by undertaking to saddle the mare. However, this should be a warning to you for the future: consider very carefully the acceptance of another trainer's problems."

"There's some awful mistake," said Katie. "Monty, I'd do it again!"

"Thanks, Katie. I'm glad it didn't rub off on you . . . whatever it is," said Monty.

"We further realize the—well, the *weird* nature of the business," went on Larry. "Three consecutive questionable or positive tests make for an enigma. But we don't believe that this oddness warrants lifting Mr. Everett's suspension at this time. We *will* investigate the chance of faulty lab procedures. Though it seems most unlikely that they'd consistently err on one horse alone, we'll do our best to check this thoroughly. Until further notice, the purse monies from both the Dresden and the Milford will be held in escrow pending a final evaluation." He looked around at them. "That's all."

Mr. Tolkov stood up slowly. True, he had vouched for Katie's absolute innocence the day before; but he had not anticipated, not truly seriously expected this disaster. "Sunbonnet," he said heavily, "will be returned to Fieldstone Farm. She will never race again."

Julie saw the room whirl around her, and shut her eyes tight for fear she would faint. Monty was dead white. Rand held Julie's hand tightly, staring at Larry O'Neill and wishing desperately for some intelligent objection to leap into his mind.

And when Drop Cord heard about it, he sat down abruptly and his eyes grew wet. "Number three," he whispered. "The worst number three I ever saw!"

The next day Julie, who had spent the night at Deepwater, with Bonnie housed in one of the great barns there, hobbled bravely into Mr. T's big office on her crutches and her all-but-useless legs. "You wanted to see me, sir?"

"Yes, dear. Sit down. I hope you realize," said the man sympathetically, "that I had no choice on Bonnie. I couldn't let her keep running after—"

"I know."

He sighed quietly. "Necessity doesn't make it easier to bear. For you or for me. But what I wanted to talk over with you is this: I need a trainer for our horses."

"Monty only has about five weeks of his suspension left. Can't Dan handle them till then?"

"I've been on the phone for hours. The Commission has extended his suspension indefinitely. One or two men told me in confidence that they believe Monty drugged the mare the first two times, under the impression that he could get away with it, and then hired someone to do it the third time so it would seem that he had nothing to do with it."

"Why, he'd have had to go out of his mind to do that, and you know it!"

"Isn't it possible that that's what he did?" Mr. T asked her as gently as he could. "I don't mean the boy's mad, I mean that worry over you, obsession with the mare's winning—"

"No!"

"Well, Julie, I won't argue that; I don't honestly cred-it it myself. The fact remains that a good many powerful men are dubious about ever allowing him near a track again. And if he can't clear himself—and how on earth can anyone prove that he did *not* drug a horse? it's about as difficult as proving that you didn't have tea with your breakfast—if he can't, though, I'll have to let him go."

"Mr. T!" she said, appalled.

"I'd have no choice. I couldn't employ a trainer who wasn't allowed on any racetrack in the country. Oh, I have nearly as much faith in Monty as you have," said Tolkov, leaning over his enormous desk. "I allow for the chance of a temporary madness, true; but on that lad's basic integrity I have no doubts whatever. I'd find him a job with Uni-Tea." That was the huge commercial complex owned by Tolkov Inc. "But it wouldn't be anything to do with racing, naturally. And I still need a trainer. You have your assistant trainer's papers. When you're better, I'd like to talk that over with you . . . I have great confidence in your abilities with horses. Meanwhile, Dan Gibson, I think, should have a chance at the job."

"You don't believe for a finger-snap that Monty went loopy and drugged her," said the girl flatly.

He looked at her steadily. "Maybe I don't. No, I think I don't. Julie, you love Monty very much, don't you?"

"Yes," said Julie promptly, startling herself momen-tarily.

"When are you going to marry him?"

"Whenever he asks me."

"What if he's barred for life? It's possible—it's even probable. And you know that racing is your life."

"It's his, too. Mr. T," said Julie, clasping her hands

together nervously, "I've asked you for a lot of favors in the past few years, and you always say yes."

"You're the only semi-adopted daughter I ever had." He smiled for the first time that day. "You've never disappointed me."

"I want you to do me a favor now that's more important than any I ever asked. It may sound pointless, hopeless, but I want you to say yes."

"I will, whatever it is."

"No, don't promise till I explain it! That isn't fair. First, please don't talk to Dan Gibson for a few days. That won't interfere with your plans, will it?"

"No rush about it. He's carrying on Monty's own regime, at any rate, he tells me."

"Then have tests run on Bonnie. I'll pay all the expenses, if you'll just agree to it and maybe pull a string or two. Let them find out if there's something *different* about her, her own self, that could make those spit-box tests come back wrong."

"That's a wild hope—"

"It's all the hope I have! And it isn't as crazy as it seems. A long shot, sure, but possible!"

"What makes you think that, Julie?" he asked, intrigued in spite of his skepticism.

"Pop Larrikin. I had a call from him, from Fieldstone, just before I got your summons. He'd been talking to Leon and Stash," the girl rattled out, so fast that his middle-aged ears had difficulty in following the words. "One of them said that they'd have to adopt Sherlock Holmes's motto: they'd eliminated the impossible (they couldn't possibly suspect Monty, Beau, Drop Cord, Marsh, Katie, any of them), so what remained *had* to be true. So what remained? Outside villains. Also just about impossible, with those track guards. Then what? And Pop remembered."

"Remembered what?" demanded Mr. T, on the edge of his chair.

"Neither Stash or Leon knew about it, but Pop did, definitely, and he doesn't imagine things. There was a case, a while back, I don't know how many years, and when it flashed into his mind Pop said he could have cussed himself out from—"

"Remembered *what?*"

"There was a horse that won and went to the spit-box and they found amphetamine. His trainer was set down. Then it happened again, and the second trained was suspended. When the horse came back positive with the third trainer, the horse was taken over lock stock and barrel by the Racing Commission. While he was in their custody, he kept on producing positive tests! There was something in his system that did it, because the Commission practically sealed him in cotton eighty-six hours a day, and they agreed that nobody could have gotten at him! So do you see why I want Bonnie experimented with?"

"Wait a second," said Mr. T, trying to quell his rising state of what he considered foolish optimism. "If that can happen, why in blazes didn't the stewards have it tested? I mean with Bonnie?"

"Because it's evidently so rare a condition that they never take it into account. Pop has only heard of the single case, and that was quite a while ago, I guess."

"What happened after they decided it was the horse's own fault?"

"The original trainer, who was also the owner, sued everyone in sight: Racing Commission, stewards, laboratory and all. There were what Pop called 'monumental stacks of lawsuits.' And he doesn't know who finally won, but at least the trainers were vindicated."

"Then, by George," said Mr. T, rising in majesty behind his desk, "we'll see that Bonnie's gone over with a fine-tooth comb! I'll have—did Pop Larrikin know where they took that horse for examination, and evaluation?"

"No."

"I'll call Skye at Kandahar; he's knowledgeable." He checked a phone list and dialed. "Sit tight, honey, we'll see about this here and now." A short wait. "That you, Doc? Rollin Tolkov. See here, the idea's been submitted that something in my mare Sunbonnet may be making her tests positive—*like* amphetamine, you know? What do you think?" Pause, while Julie held her breath. "Never heard of such a thing? Well, neither had I, but a man who works for me has, and he—what?" Mr. T laughed outright. "Great geldings and goldfish! Does everyone in the world know Leon Pitt? No, it wasn't. Pop Larrikin. There was such a case, some time ago." He listened for quite a while. He made notes on a pad. "I'll do it. What? Oh, the owner sued everyone in creation." Another chortle. Mr. T was feeling better. Like Julie, he loved to look on the sunny side, even when the odds were fantastically against him. "Don't worry, I won't sue, but if she *should* be that one-in-a-million freak of nature, Larry O'Neill's going to buy Monty Everett the best dinner in town, Doc!" He rang off.

"Well?" Julie breathed.

"Two places we can send her to check this out. Closest is Cornell University, in upstate New York."

"Oh, could we van her up soon?"

"No," said Rollin Tolkov absently, looking through a phone book.

"I'll gladly pay—"

"You will not. This is my outfit and my fight. I'm going to send her up there by plane."

"You're wonderful, Mr. T."

"I'm the doggone salt of the earth. We're likely making fools of ourselves, Julie. We oughtn't to let our enthusiasm start running high. But it's so good to find a spark of something besides doom and misery in this whole affair that we're helpless before it. *I* hope. The shine in your eye says that *you* hope. Very well! We hope!" he shouted, clapping his hands twice like a conjurer. "They'll be calling us Pollyanna and Mr. Micawber! I don't care, I suddenly feel that the whole thing has to be solved; therefore, it will be solved. Monty didn't do anything wrong. We'll prove it. The same goes for Beau and Drop Cloth."

"Drop Cord!" she laughed.

"Oh? Some day you must tell me what that odd name means. However, to business! We are now going to speak to Cornell, and throw around our considerable weight." He patted his rotund stomach. "And if we're riding for a nasty fall, at least we're doing it with high spirits and vigor!"

He dialed the phone.

Chapter *TWELVE*

Because the stairs of her Deepwater apartment were difficult for Julie to negotiate, her father took her home to the Fieldstone cottage that afternoon. The following day, Bonnie was flown up to the university under the care and with the affectionate company of her old friend Monty, whom she had not seen in much too long.

In contrast to the glorious weather at Kandahar and Deepwater, it had been raining slowly and steadily here for the better part of two weeks. Without the now-buoyant presence of Mr. T, and with the untypically mournful faces of her friends on the breeding farm (all of whom, even Pop, considered this new investigation—in the words of Stash—a wild-horse chase), as well as the glowering weather, Julie found herself sliding back into melancholy once more. She tried to extend her exercise period, but was so weary after all the emotions and discomfort of riding that she only made herself ill, and had to go to bed in mid-afternoon.

Next morning the sun was shining, rather diluted by some humid-looking clouds, and Julie dressed and swung slowly outside to visit the twins. As yearlings, they were no longer turned out in a field together, but with their peers: the colt with colts, the filly with fillies. For Julie's sake, while she waited to hear about Bonnie, they had been brought down and put into adjacent paddocks near her cottage, so that she could visit them easily and feel less lonesome.

The first thing she heard as she approached the nearest paddock was a whimpering neigh from Deerstalker, the colt. He was shifting around near the fence, tossing his head and showing the whites of his eyes. "What is it, boy?" she called, coming up to the fence. He glared at her as though she were a stranger; though only yesterday he had been delighted to frolic with her.

Julie glanced over at the next paddock. It was on slightly rolling ground, but it seemed to be empty. She walked as quickly as she could to a vantage point from which she could see the whole enclosure. Tam, the filly, was not there. Julie called her name a little anxiously. There was no sound but another neigh from Deer.

Julie went down to where a gate swung open that should have been closed. Hurriedly or carelessly fastened, the filly must have managed to shove it free and wandered off. Perhaps she'd gone across country to the fillies' field where she'd been accustomed to play. . . .

The girl bent over, angling her crutches carefully. The freshest hoofprints in the soggy ground aimed toward the river, almost due north. Deer whinnied loudly. Julie straightened herself and looked at him: he began to "run the fence line"—dashing along the barrier for a hundred yards or so, stopping in his tracks, thrusting his head over the wooden post and calling, racing back to repeat the performance at his starting point.

The twins were no longer so intimately friendly that they had to be near each other. Was Tam in danger, and did Deer know it in that uncanny way of communication that animals have? Julie bit her knuckle, scowling.

There was no danger on this whole vast farm for a young horse, but perhaps Deer's instincts were sounder than Julie's common sense. Or maybe he could hear something that she couldn't.

Without further hesitation, the girl gait-walked over a rise and laid a halting course northward. She hurried as fast as her almost useless legs would allow her, but as the ground grew mucky nearer the river, her crutches slid and threatened to go out of control, and she had to slow even her crippled pace.

"This is dumb," she said aloud. "I ought to go get Dad or somebody who has two good legs. I couldn't get her back in if I did find her."

Then, as Deer shut up for a moment, she heard plainly from someplace in front of her the high-pitched yell of a young horse in trouble. She want on, past a ragged grove of trees, and saw where the steady rains had so saturated the riverbank area that, weakening the already disintegrating limestone that underlies the fertile loam of the Bluegrass region, they had created a few more sinkholes and pits. From the nearest of these came the thrashing, squealing, terrified noises that Deer must have heard long before Julie did.

"Tam!" Julie hurried as best she could do the brink of the depression. It was indeed freshly made, perhaps a dozen feet across, almost six deep. Tam, the filly, was a poor, muddy, white-eyed object at the bottom; struggling up, kicking, nickering, sliding down again, whirling clumsily around, drawing lips back from teeth in mindless fear. "Tam, darling Tam, I'm here!" Julie moved as close to the edge as she dared and began to talk soothingly, but the beast was frantic.

The girl could not help the filly, it was obvious to her in a moment. She needed at least a couple of strong men. Turning to head back to the barns, she put her crutches down on apparently solid earth that sank in beneath the weight; she jerked at them in sudden panic, another section of the sinkhole rim sloughed off into the pit, and carried a screaming Julie down with it.

The filly twisted round, neighed dreadfully, and reared on her hind legs to kick the air above the girl lying prostrate in the muck.

Rand Jefferson walked out of the cottage, talking earnestly with Stash Watkins. "Whatever happens," said the latter moodily, "I just wish that Monty would marry the girl and settle down and give up all his riotous ways."

Rand chuckled. Then he caught Stash's arm and said, "Hey, look at that colt!"

"What's he runnin' the fence line for?" Both men ran toward Deerstalker's paddock. The colt had increased his screeching ruckus and was lathered, dripping with sweat, and quite uncontrollable. Stash went into the enclosure and did his best to calm the horse, who would not be cooled down. Rand meantime, in peering about for his daughter, discovered that Tam was missing.

"Stash, I'm going to look for Julie and the filly," he called. Stash, his hands full, nodded.

Julie was in terror for both herself and the maddened filly. This tiny hole in the riverbank was not big enough to hold them both unless they stayed very still; but Tam persisted in making circuits of the pit, flexing herself and rearing and pivoting and slewing around while making the most awful clamor Julie had ever heard.

"Tam, Tam dear, there's a good girl, be quiet, Tam," Julie said, and was abashed at how much her voice sounded like a whimper. Tam made a desperate attempt to climb one slippery side, kicking out in all directions.

Julie untangled herself as best she could. The bands on her crutches, which fitted below the elbow, had twisted but were still on her arms; she gripped the things tremulously, maneuvered sideways, and somehow struggled to her feet. The filly kicked her heels high and whirled round and round in a frightful parody of a young horse at play.

The slippery earth was a trap for Julie's crutch tips and her feet, and there was nothing to hang onto in this dismal hole except the bank. The girl smashed herself flat against this, mire on her face and her blond hair, dirt in her eyes and between her lips; if there were something solid to grip, she might haul herself out, if she could stand on tiptoe—*if if if!* Willing her dead legs to hold her up, she reached toward the edge of the steep bank.

There was a smashing blow on her back, and the world dropped with a spasm of torment and a sound like a horse's neigh into the dark of oblivion.

Stash came out of the paddock and trotted toward Rand, who was reading the spoor of Julie's crutches in the damp ground. "That colt gonna have to go in and be thoroughly wrung out and dried off pretty soon," he said, walking beside Rand.

"Need any help?"

"After we see what Julie's up to."

"Do you hear anything?" asked Rand.

They both listened. "Only that fool colt. Gone loco! I hope it's nothin' to do with Julie."

"Oh, I'm sure it isn't. But let's follow this trail."

"And maybe holler a little?" suggested Stash.

"Wouldn't hurt."

"Cause nothin's gonna scare that Deerstalker boy any more than he's spooked now. Hey, Julie!"

They both shouted her name, and went toward the river.

Julie came to herself instantaneously, passing from blackness to full awareness of her surroundings. She had been unconscious, though of course she did not know it, for only about two minutes.

She remembered that she had been trying to climb out. She clawed her way out of the tangled huddle of her own limbs and the metal crutches, and saw that the filly was standing quiet for the moment, either through fatigue or because Julie's stillness had scared her into immobility. The girl got to her feet, her back writhing with pain, and after leaning on the steep slope of the bank for a few seconds, gritting her teeth and rubbing her eyes free of mud and tears, she looked up at the rim of the sinkhole. A medium-sized tree root thrust out of the earth on a level with Julie's face, a foot or so below ground level. It was directly across the pit from her. She had not noticed it before because the horse had blocked her view.

Julie took two or three short steps toward it and slid and fell to her knees. It was not until she had clambered to her feet again that she realized she had not been using her crutches. She still wore them, but she had walked unaided, on her own two legs!

She stood swaying dizzily in the center of the little crater, bewildered and more frightened, perhaps, than before. What had happened? How had she moved forward by herself? Her legs were useless.

She looked down at them, incredulous. Slowly she took off the crutches; gripping one in either hand, using them as canes, she went past the filly, moving her legs as though it had been nine weeks ago and no accident had ever occurred.

She heard groaning: it came from her own lips. Her spinal column was full of fire. Could she have wrenched it when she fell into the pit? No, it hadn't been hurting too badly before she tried to climb out. . . .

Tam turned her head and regarded Julie with a dull, forlorn eyeball.

"Wait a minute," said Julie, eyeing her back. "Did you kick me, by any chance? I was reaching up, and the universe exploded, and then I stood up and started to walk. It was like—like amnesia! I forgot for a minute that I couldn't walk." She was about to reach out and pat the horse, but held back for fear the touch would start Tam off on her panicky activity again. "Did you kick me in the back? It felt like a sledgehammer hit me —I wonder if you knocked those two vertebrae off the nerve, or vice versa? I can feel my legs, and move them! They're holding me up! *Some*thing happened, honey, and I really think it was you!"

Aching abominably, Julie took another step, tossed her crutches up over the rim, grasped the root and drew herself up. Clawing at muddy earth and rocks and the root, she hauled herself inch by inch off the floor of the sinkhole. Her arms, more powerful than ever before in her life because of the weeks of exercise and crutch-walking, pulled her slim body upward until she was lying on her face, half out of the dreadful cavity. After a brief rest, she wriggled her legs up and sideways and she was out, on the blessed muddy miserable soggy world above the pit.

It was there that Rand and Stash found her a minute later, crying for pure joy of the tingles and pangs in her wakened legs.

Julie lay in the hospital bed and thought thankful thoughts.

Rand had called the doctor as soon as he'd carried Julie down to the cottage on his back, while Stash went flying for help from the stables to rescue Tam and clean up Deer after his emotional binge of running the fence line. The Doctor had said to bring her in *now*. Making her comfortable on the broad back seat of a borrowed station wagon, Rand had barreled off to Chambers Memorial.

The first thing that the physician ascertained was that Tam had indeed kicked her squarely on the spine, just at the place where that first wild hoof had caught her. The bruise was so definitely hoof-shaped that no other explanation was needed. Even before he had ordered X-rays and a therapist's check, the doctor told her, "It wasn't exactly a miracle, you know, unless a lucky accident can be called miraculous. One hoof undid what another caused. The pressure's off that nerve, you can be sure, or you wouldn't be able to work those legs. I'll see you when the tests have been made."

So now she lay here, slightly sedated for the pain, waiting confidently for his report. Rand was reading a book in an armchair by the window. Julie began to doze.

The doctor came in. He was smiling.

"It's good, then," said Julie, waking up.

"Well, I'm going to keep you here overnight, just to get you some solid rest for the shock and the pain, but you can go home tomorrow at noon or so. You'll have to wear that brace for a little while. Not long. Just till your back's used to being itself again."

"When can I ride?" she demanded.

He chuckled. "Not for a while, my dear; but, again, not too long a period, I'd guess, before you're in the saddle again. Horses have certainly caused you a lot of grief lately—"

"Not on purpose!"

"But now one's gone and fixed you up, neater than I could have done it. The vertebrae are in their proper place. All the life's flowed back into your legs, to put it in layman's talk."

"No operation," said Julie gratefully. "No chance of being on crutches for life."

"No, indeed! With the brace, and favoring your body till it's quite normal, and remembering to be careful about turning your back on horses from now on, you'll soon have no residual effects whatever."

"Doctor," said Rand thoughtfully, "when you first prescribed for her case, you said absolutely no manipulation. It seems to me that a crack from a horse's hoof is about the ultimate in 'manipulation,' yet it worked."

"I was going to mention that," said the medical man. "At the beginning, and again when she had those four-week X-rays, manipulation was contraindicated." He grinned at Julie's frown. "Inadvisable! The proximity of the two vertebrae to the spinal cord made anything beyond therapy quite dangerous. Since then, however, you've made great progress, obviously you've stuck hard to your regimen; and the proximity of displaced vertebrae to spinal cord had become less critical. I think that it wouldn't have been too long before we'd have tried manipulation. However, the way it did happen to you, Julie, was—well, as if I'd closed my eyes and taken a swing at your back with a mallet. Somewhat unorthodox! One chance in a thousand say. You've been very lucky."

"Thank God," said Rand devoutly.

"Amen," said Julie.

When they had been alone for a while, and her father believed that she was dozing again, Julie said in a hushed voice, "I wonder if that's about the odds for Bonnie—one in a thousand? I hope that's all. With only one case before that anyone knows about, do you think I'm ridiculously sunny to think Bonnie may be the second?"

"You mean, maybe you ought to have let her be retired without a fight to the ultimate ditch?"

"I guess that's what I mean, yes."

"The day you do that in any situation, you'll have stopped being Julie Jefferson. *Always* fight to the end. Never give up. That's your creed, and it makes you who you are."

"Mr. T works that way, too. I suppose it's not a bad plan."

"I can name a legion of worse ones."

"What if Bonnie's just perfectly normal? What will I do?"

"Hire private detectives to find out the chance of some enemy of yours or Monty's being responsible," he said promptly. "I remember some tough mugs that you two sent to jail a few years ago. Not everyone in racing loves and honors a top winner like Bonnie, either. There's plenty you can do before we give up."

"Right," she said, and drifted off to sleep. Rand left her alone, and put in a call to Rollin Tolkov at Deepwater Farm.

Monty had not yet returned with the mare from the north. But Mr. T was jubilant at the news of Julie's incredible recovery, and instantly determined that he would give a getting-well party for her in the great dining hall of Deepwater the following evening. "We'll have all her friends in," he said, "at least, as many as we can fit into the place!"

Chapter **THIRTEEN**

In the teeth of all Rand's opposition, Julie insisted on riding back to Fieldstone the next afternoon, although it would mean a good many miles of extra travel for her.

"My back is fine with the brace—we can pick up the gang and take them all to Deepwater for Mr. T's party —and I have to show the puppies that I'm better!"

"That's a little whimsical, I must say," Rand suggested. "Do you think they'll know the difference? They love you afoot, in the saddle, or stretched out helpless; they don't make distinctions."

"Nana does."

Rand considered. "Yes, you're right. The way she put away all her toys, and turned herself into a sentry by your bed . . ."

"And I must thank Tam, and Deer for warning me to go look for her. Please?"

"Okay, Julie. But if you're overly tired tonight, and fall asleep in the middle of the baked Alaska, don't say I didn't warn you."

She survived the long trip to Fieldstone splendidly, and walked with her father's arm supporting her from the wagon to the cottage. Pushy and Nana came to the door as they opened it. Pushy offered his huge head gravely to be petted, but Nana danced and spun and could not be calm long enough to have her ears scratched. At last she stood in the center of the living room, tail going furiously, and appeared to remember something of great importance. She whipped around and dove in behind the overstuffed chair that always sat beside the bookcase. There was the sound of scrabbling as she pawed through her toys, and then she marched out with an ancient beef bone in her jaws. This she solemnly offered to Julie, who bent rather stiffly and accepted it. Nana zoomed back and brought out, one by one, all her precious possessions, scattering them through the house with evident care and thought for just where each one belonged.

"Life resumes itself, and all is normal once more," said Rand. "That is amazing, Julie. The beagle did know how wrong things were with you, and now she sees or senses that you're better. That's just as extraordinary a pup as you've always claimed."

"Wait till Leon hears about this! He'll never dare insult her intelligence again."

After half an hour's rest, Julie walked over to the barn and found her gang, and the jubilation was riotous. Tam and Deer had recovered from their ordeals and were playing happily in the yearling fields. Everything was back to normal, and the relief over Julie's vertebrae was such that Bonnie was never once mentioned, although more than one man had the quick and rueful thought that once her delight at the unexpected recovery faded a little, distress over her mare, the light of her life, would return as deep as ever. Pop Larrikin, indeed, found himself wishing that he'd never mentioned that old and forgotten case: what good did it do to raise hopes over such a ramshackle prospect? But Julie had told him at the time that she'd decided to have the Deepwater vet run blood tests and intensive examinations. "She'd have been just as pepped over that," he told himself angrily. "Let be, you old worry wart! Even the longest shot in the world has to be taken when there's nothing else to try!"

At four o'clock, after a nap, Julie dressed in her finest and with her father, Leon Pitt, Pop, and Stash, set out for Deepwater. She was restrained with some difficulty from taking the beagle along to show off and brag about.

"Mighty nice of Mr. Tolkov to ask a bunch of old stable hands out to dine with him," said Leon. "Even the celebrated fraternity of the track doesn't often go this far."

"He knows I wouldn't feel it was a real party without you three," said Julie. "And you know that Mr. T considers every groom and exercise boy as a member of his family."

"That's why he gets such fine work and loyalty out of all his crews," said Stash. "And I bet a month's pay he's the only millionaire that does, too. I know *I'd* sweat my fingers to the bone for him."

"The day you show any bone peepin' through those soft and untouched fingers, grampaw," said Leon caustically, "is the day that I dye my hair and become a star of stage, screen, and television."

"I can work you into the ground with a bunch o' daisies on top of you any time you want to compete," said Stash.

"Do you two always argue like this?" asked Rand, grinning.

"Who's arguing? I merely use the poor old soul to hone my wit against," said Leon.

"Wittiest dude in the stable," said Stash, "right next to Pushy and Tweedy."

"Tweedy's got plenty of wit," retorted Leon. "I saw him trying to kick you yesterday when you were workin' so hard you'd gone to sleep in his stall."

"That wasn't wit," said Stash, sinking back comfortably in his seat. "That was broad slapstick humor, like a certain ancient foreman's I could mention."

"You two!" said Pop. "Hope and Crosby in *The Road to Deepwater.*"

"Little too sunburned for that impersonation," said Leon, a vast grin engulfing his face. "Say, do you suppose the lot of us really smell like a round-up of horses, or is my embarrassed imagination working overtime?"

"We probably do," said Julie. "Mr. T won't mind, he likes horses."

Rand, driving quietly, wondered whether the pair were doing their best to keep his girl's mind off the issue of Bonnie. He was grateful and rather surprised that it hadn't come up. Julie's mind must be full of it.

As it happened, Julie was not even thinking of her great bay mare; having decided that she would go on investigating the case as long as a single avenue of feasibility remained, she had managed to put it out of her head. The relief of walking free again was still strong in her, helping to get her through these hours.

At Deepwater they found Drop Cord, looking very strange and imposing in a jacket and slacks—none of them had ever seen him out of his work clothes, for Drop Cord put in a seven-day week all year round—as well as Beau and Dan Gibson.

"Monty . . . ?" asked Julie.

"Haven't seen him. Thought he'd be with you," said Beau.

Mr. T rolled into the big dining room, where they had all been brought by a waiter. "Sit down, all of you! Monty will be with us in a minute. Julie, I haven't told him about your recovery; I thought that should be your privilege."

"You mean Monty's been away somewhere?" said Drop Cord.

"Cornell University," said Mr. T, seating Julie and then himself. "For the three of you who don't know about this development, maybe Pop would run through the facts in the case he recollected."

The three track men turned as one toward Pop, who reddened at being in the spotlight and dashed off what he knew of the horse that had been its own worst enemy.

Drop Cord struck himself on the forehead. "Why didn't I remember! All this time and I never once thought of it!" he shouted; then looked abashed at bawling out like that in this gilded hall of wealth and culture.

Mr. T chuckled. "I gather it's such a rarity, Drop Kick, that nobody would have recollected it offhand."

"Drop Cord," said Julie in his ear.

But Drop Cord had not noticed. *"I* should have! I don't know about this horse Pop speaks of, but there was another one like it in England. It happened when I was travelin' with Dr. Lejeune; we were over there and it was in the regular newspapers, even—the horse's own system did it! What was the word? Steroids! Steroids showed in his own system! Fouled up the tests just like Bonnie's were."

"Well," said Pop, brightening, "that's two, and maybe it's not all that rare. Maybe there's hope."

"One case for me and one for you," said Drop Cord, "that's pretty scarce evidence, Pop, considerin' we've been around the track for about eighty years between us."

"Still, it sure was log-stupid not to remember it before, much as we've all been worrying about it," said Beau severely. "I'm ashamed of you, D.C."

"Not as ashamed of me as I am." The big man shook his head. "So long ago, though . . . is that why Monty went to Cornell?"

"He took Bonnie up for tests, yes. They flew back this afternoon," said Mr. T.

"And?"

"He'll tell us. He only came into the house when he'd seen the mare settled, and I made him go and clean up before saying a word." Their boss looked around the table at them. "No, I don't know any more than you do. And I'm wasting away with wonder, too. But he'll clear it up when he comes in."

"Didn't he even phone you when the tests were done?" asked Julie blankly.

"No, I'd told him to save it. To come back with the news himself."

"Mr. T, do you enjoy sitting on the point of a thumbtack for a day longer than necessary?" the girl demanded.

He regarded her steadily. "No. I simply couldn't face the prospect of breaking your heart by proxy—of telling you we'd failed in person, without a lot of people to cushion the disappointment. So, cowardly, I called this gathering and left it to Monty."

She smiled slightly. "I don't believe that at all."

"I can face a board room full of powerful and financially dangerous men and quell 'em with a word," said Mr. T, "but face your tears, Julie? No."

"You wanted to wait till Monty'd come home because you believe as much as I do that it's going to be the answer—that it's a mistake in a laboratory, and not a crooked deal by a friend—and you wanted it to be Monty who'd tell me."

"Oh, well," said Mr. T, hiding his face momentarily

behind a gigantic dinner napkin, "perhaps that was part of it. Well, at any rate, here's the young fellow now, shaved and decently clad, to tell us. Welcome home, Monty. Sit here."

The trainer walked steadily over to the chair on Mr. T's left and sat down. His face could not be read; it was perfectly composed.

"Hi, everybody. Julie, you look great, but aren't you a little pale?"

"Montgomery Everett, you cut that out!" she cried.

"Or I'll bust you one," added Stash.

"Well," he said, leaning back. "Well, we have ourselves a racehorse. We've won. We're all vindicated."

Pandemonium.

Julie stood up and walked around her boss's chair and put out her hands to Monty. "Oh, dear Monty," she said, eyes moist, "thank you."

"All I did was go along with her."

Then he stood up and put his hands on her shoulders. "I'm more happy for you than I am for me," he said, "and I'm *very* happy for me." He gazed down at her face. Then his own expression changed. "Where are your crutches? What's happened?"

"Oh, that," said Julie. "I was kicked by another horse." She walked around him in a little circle. "Good as new in a few days."

He couldn't speak, but he made noises of rejoicing; and then somehow they were in each other's arms and Monty was kissing Julie, who was kissing him back, and a spontaneous cheer rose from around the table, which neither of them noticed.

"Now he has to marry the girl!" crowed Stash happily.

Rand said to Mr. T, "That's why you didn't tell either of them anything, you old schemer. Why you wouldn't let Monty break his news to anyone till now."

"Well, that's possible," said Mr. T, beaming.

"Even if he'd had bad news, it would have worked out," said Rand. "Julie'd have felt so sorry for him, having to tell her; and he'd have been so torn between despair and jubilation over her recovery that the bars would all have come down anyway."

"If enough emotion was let loose, I rather thought this had a chance to happen," said Mr. T. "It's long overdue. I think they've loved each other for years."

"Since they were kids, really," said Rand.

"Julie," said Monty, unaware that anyone else was within hearing distance, "when are you going to marry me?"

"When you ask me," said Julie, breathless.

"I'm asking you!"

"All right, Monty dear, I'll marry you. I've wanted to be your wife for years."

"You have? Why didn't you say any——"

"Why didn't you?"

They stared at each other. "Do you suppose we were too busy with horses?" he asked.

"And with growing up."

"It certainly took us long enough to do that!"

"Some people *never* make it. Monty, kiss me?"

He did so.

"On the count of three," said Rollin Tolkov in a stage whisper, "another good loud cheer. Ready? One, two, three!"

The triumphant shout was like a miniature reproduction of the crowd's roar whenever Sunbonnet crossed a finish line. The young man and the girl broke apart, both of them blushing and laughing. Mr. T stood and insisted that Julie take his chair, so she would be next to Monty. Seating himself in another, he said, "Now, before the food comes, tell us about it, Monty."

"Nothing much to tell. I asked her to marry me, and she said——"

"Everybody heard that," said Drop Cord, "that's old stuff now. What about Bonnie?"

"Bonnie," said Monty as though the name was strange to him. "Oh, Bonnie! But I want to hear how Julie's legs got better so quickly."

"I said I was kicked by a horse," she told him, and in a few sentences explained about Tam. "Now your news."

Monty took a gulp of water. "Okay, I went up there with Bonnie, never dreaming that there was a chance of discovering a solid reason for those positive tests. I was still trying to sort out the culprit or culprits in my mind." He looked at Drop Cord and Beau. "You know, you two both made noises before the Marquesa about how you'd do anything to make Bonnie win, and Beau was so mysterious about that errand he had to run . . . you take away a fellow's license to earn his living and leave him alone, far away from the track, for long enough, and he'll start suspecting his grandmother, let alone two of his best friends."

"We both did the same thing," said Drop Cord, shamfaced. "About you."

"That stupid errand," grumbled Beau. "I couldn't tell you about that, Monty: it was such a nice idea at the time, and then when the troubles began, it woulda seemed crazy."

"What?"

"I was workin' on two presents, one for you, one for Julie. They came in just about the time the Dresden test turned up positive. Well, I couldn't have given 'em to you *then,* could I? You didn't want to be reminded of the Marquesa any more'n necessary."

"What presents?" asked Leon.

"Where I went, which Monty remembered afterwards

and asked me and I wouldn't tell him, right before the race, was to the offices of Racing Monitor, the film company, which were in a mobile unit at the track."

"Film company?" asked Rand, as the others nodded comprehension.

"They're responsible for all the films of all the races, both the permanent variety and the instant replays," said Julie.

"I'm friends with a couple of the guys on their crew, and I was makin' final arrangements for these gifts for Julie and Monty. They were gonna let me have stills, what-d'you-call-'ems, blowups, from frames of the movie, of Bonnie in strategic points of the race. Then I was gonna make a layout of these—starting with the break from the gate, then her position at the quarter pole, the half, the top of the stretch, and her finish all alone—grouped around the win photo in the center. Which I did. Then I took them to another friend of mine who does work like this, and had 'em matted and framed, and below the win photo it says, 'Sunbonnet,' and her sire and dam's names, and the names of the owner, trainer, and jockey, whoever they might be; and 'Marquesa Stakes,' and the date, and her time. They're about two feet square, and they look great. But I got 'em four days after the Dresden, and they gave me the willies, so I just put 'em in my apartment. All wrapped up neat."

"Oh, Beau, you're a wonderful friend!" Said Julie.

"I guess you'll only be wanting one of them now, though," said the jockey, smiling. "I think I'll give the other to Mr. Tolkov, who's a really great boss."

"In honor of the dinner he's going to give us all when you've finished talkin' at such vast lengths," said Stash to his son.

"Beau," said Mr. T, "I'd be grateful for one of them. I'll give it the place of honor in my office here. Sunbonnet's comeback race."

"That's why I thought of 'em in the first place," said Beau. "Because naturally I knew she was gonna win."

"So did I," said Drop Cord wrly, "too darn well. Monty, go on."

"I don't like to hold up dinner, making a speech—"

"Mr. Everett, *tell,*" said Rollin Tolkov, "or I won't give you that raise I'm planning as a wedding gift."

"Yes sir. We went to Cornell," said Monty, trying to include everyone but unable to keep his eyes off a radiant Julie, "and they ran samples of everything, blood, urine, saliva, and for all I know, lymph and sweat, through their mass spectrograph. There are only two of those in the country, because they're enormously expensive. When they'd separated everything, they found that Bonnie does have a substance in her that tests out like amphetamine."

"Wow!" said Pop irrespressibly.

"That's right. In her basic metabolic processes, Bonnie is producing a substance, or substances, that test out *like* amphetamine, though that drug was ruled out completely, thank heaven; and any time you test her, morning, evening, before or after racing, she'll test like amphetamine."

Mr. T said, "How can this be? Why did she never show that before the Marquesa?"

"I can't answer that," said Monty, "but it may have something to do with the fact that in the interim she foaled, and foaled twins at that: a rare occurrence, an even rarer result. Her metabolism has changed."

Rand asked, "Why couldn't they have discovered this at the racing lab?"

"Racetrack lab tests are fair at best," said Monty, and Mr. T nodded vigorously. "They have an ultraviolet spectrograph; so their tests aren't perfect, it isn't possible to make them perfect because of the cost, but in most cases they're accurate enough. Bonnie's case is extraordinary, but not unique."

"While you were away," said Leon, "we did hear of a similar instance in England." Drop Cord looked at the ceiling and pretended to find its pattern fascinating.

"After all," Monty said, "the ultraviolet spectrograph is nowhere near the mass spectrograph—"

"Bet you can't say that again fast," murmured Julie.

"And the Racing Commission only has access to the ultraviolet. Masks do exist, which can obscure, obliterate, or confuse a test: if a horse is drugged, for instance, massive doses of a B vitamin will camouflage the forbidden substance. But this was a case of something showing up unmasked and pretending to be a drug when it really isn't at all."

"It was steroids showed in that English horse's system," said Drop Cord. "I'm abashed I didn't bring it to mind sooner."

"It wouldn't have proved a thing," said Monty. "We needed the mass spectrograph to prove it."

"One question."

"Yes, Stash?"

"What in the blue-eyed world *is* a mass specter photograph, or whatever? Sounds like a picture of a convention of ghosts."

"I was hoping someone would ask that," said Monty happily. "It's an apparatus, phenomenally expensive, that separates a stream of charged particles into a spectrum, according to the masses of the particles, using magnetic and electrical fields."

"One more question. What did you just say?"

"I'm not really sure. I memorized that. But it's given us our Bonnie back," said Monty.

"Did you get the analysis and all the facts in writing up there?" Mr. T asked him.

"I sure did." Monty rubbed his jaw thoughtfully. "I didn't imagine that the stewards and the Commission would just take my word for it."

"Nor the blasted *Daily Herald,* which is going to print the facts of the matter as soon as I can speak to the editor, together with an apology, a retraction, and a glowing account of Sunbonnet's entire career—Sunbonnet the Wonder Horse!—complete with photographs," said Mr. T. He gave a sign to a waiter, who hurried kitchenward.

"Are you sure?" Julie whispered to Monty.

"I always have been! Are you?"

"Yes, dear. Poor Dirk! I think he was ready to ask me, and I kept hoping that you'd say something first. And you did."

"He can be head of the ushers, whatever that's called. Your dad will give you away, naturally, but who'll be best man? I can't decide. We owe them all so much— Stash, Leon, Beau, Drop Cord, there never was a better set of friends."

"Make them draw straws," whispered Mr. T.

Drop Cord laid a hand on Beau's shoulder; the former was considerably larger than the latter, and practically swallowed it. "Threes!" said the big man, winking protentously. "Didn't I say it? Three disasters as plain as day, and now three great things happen in a row. Julie's fixed up and can walk, Bonnie's in the clear and rarin' to go on, and the marriage of the year is about to take place."

"Drop Cord, your system has broken down at last," said Beau soberly. "You gotta find another superstition to lean on. Because a fourth good occurrence is ready to burst upon us this minute."

"What? What are you saying, little fellow? They always come by threes!" said the other indignantly.

"Okay, but figure out how come there's *four* this

time," said Beau. "Maybe everything's gonna be good from now on? I guess that's it. One set of three goods right after another."

"What fourth thing?" demanded Drop Cord.

"It's comin' through that door this minute, on about a hundred silver platters," said Beau happily. "The supper of the century!"

Other SIGNET Books You Will Enjoy

☐ **LISA, BRIGHT AND DARK by John Neufeld.** Lisa is slowly going mad but her symptoms—even an attempted suicide—fail to alert her parents or teachers to her illness. She finds compassion only from three girlfriends who band together to provide what they call "group therapy." (#Y6627—$1.25)

☐ **FOR ALL THE WRONG REASONS by John Neufeld.** From the bestselling author of **Lisa, Bright and Dark** comes a tender, taut novel about a teen-age marriage that speaks to today. (#W7321—$1.50)

☐ **I'VE MISSED A SUNSET OR THREE by Phyllis Anderson Wood.** Rachel and Jim just didn't care about anything—school, friends, family—not even themselves. And then they met each other. . . . (#Y7944—$1.25)

☐ **THE STORY OF SANDY by Susan Stanhope Wexler.** The moving true story of a foster parent's courageous fight for the sanity of a deeply disturbed little boy. (#W8012—$1.50)

☐ **WHERE THE LILIES BLOOM by Vera and Bill Cleaver.** In the tradition of **True Grit** and **Sounder**, this poignant, delightful novel is about a 14-year-old who vows to hold her family together against all odds. With 8 pages of photos from the triumphant motion picture! (#W8065—$1.50)

THE NEW AMERICAN LIBRARY, INC.,
P.O. Box 999, Bergenfield, New Jersey 07621

Please send me the SIGNET BOOKS I have checked above. I am enclosing $_____(check or money order—no currency or C.O.D.'s). Please include the list price plus 35¢ a copy to cover handling and mailing costs. (Prices and numbers are subject to change without notice.)

Name_____

Address_____

City_____State_____Zip Code_____
Allow at least 4 weeks for delivery

SIGNET Young Adult Titles by Phyllis A. Whitney

More Books from SIGNET You'll Want to Read

☐ **PAPER MOON by Joe David Brown.** Travel with the most charming heroine since **True Grit,** as eleven-year-old con artist Addie roams the back roads of the Depression South giving the business to all the fools she meets along the way. A major Paramount Picture starring Tatum and Ryan O'Neal. (#W7448—$1.50)

☐ **FAIR WITH RAIN by Ann Head.** A wonderfully warm and entertaining novel about a delightful South Carolina family you'll wish were yours. "Recommended . . . a pleasant and shrewdly observed family, you can't help liking them."—**Chicago Sunday Tribune**

(#Q5526—95¢)

☐ **MR. AND MRS. BO JO JONES by Ann Head.** A deeply moving story of two courageous teenagers caught in a marriage of necessity. (#W7869—$1.50)

☐ **TRUE GRIT by Charles Portis.** A widely-acclaimed novel, set in the 1870's, about a spunky fourteen-year-old girl out to avenge her father's death and the mean and tough U.S. Marshal who befriends her.

(#Y5419—$1.25)

☐ **LISTEN TO THE SILENCE by David W. Elliott.** A total and unique experience—gripping, poignant, most often, shattering. A fourteen-year-old boy narrates the chronicle of events that lead him into, through, and out of an insane asylum. (#Y6588—$1.25)